A Serendipitous Error

Ivan Goncharov

A Serendipitous Error

Translated by Stephen Pearl

Followed by

An Evil Malady

Reproach. Explanation. Farewell

Translated by Roger Cockrell

ALMA CLASSICS

ALMA CLASSICS
an imprint of

ALMA BOOKS LTD
Thornton House
Thornton Road
Wimbledon Village
London SW19 4NG
United Kingdom
www.almaclassics.com

A Serendipitous Error, first published in Russian in 1839
Translation © Stephen Pearl, 2023

An Evil Malady first published in Russian in 1838
Reproach. Explanation. Farewell first published in Russian in 1843
Translation © Roger Cockrell, 2023

This collection first published by Alma Classics in 2023

Cover: Nathan Burton

Notes © Alma Books Ltd

Printed in Great Britain by CPI Group (UK) Ltd, Croydon CR0 4YY

ISBN: 978-1-84749-911-0

Contents

A Serendipitous Error

Table of Ranks

Civil Service	Military	Court
1) Chancellor	Field Marshal/ Admiral	
2) Active Privy Councillor	General	Chief Chamberlain
3) Privy Councillor	Lieutenant General	Marshal of the House
4) Active State Councillor	Major General	Chamberlain
5) State Councillor	Brigadier	Master of Ceremonies
6) Collegiate Councillor	Colonel	Chamber Fourrier
7) Court Councillor	Lieutenant Colonel	
8) Collegiate Assessor	Major	House Fourrier
9) Titular Councillor	Staff Captain	
10) Collegiate Secretary	Lieutenant	
11) Ship Secretary*	*Kammerjunker*	
12) Government Secretary	Sub-Lieutenant	
13) Provincial Secretary*		
14) Collegiate Registrar	Senior Ensign	

*   *(abolished in 1834)*

A Serendipitous Error

A SERENDIPITOUS ERROR

(1839)

"DEAR GOD!... There is already so much trouble on this earth... why did you have to go and flood it with women?"* Gogol

"Went into one room – found myself in another."* Griboyedov

One winter at twilight... Oh yes! Before I continue, I should ask you if you like the twilight. I hear silence. Since silence means consent, I'll take it that you do. Is it only a traveller who has lost his way who is horrified by it? A thrifty shopkeeper, whether or not he has had a good day, is always in a bad mood at closing time; a painter who has not succeeded in depicting his cherished dream on canvas throws down his brush in disgust, and the poet up in his garret showers curses on Apollo the shopkeeper, who doesn't make a free gift of his candles. Everyone else welcomes this time of the day – not to mention the common people, the tradesmen and workmen who earn their bread by the sweat of their brow and lay down their tools after a hard day's work, and the seamstresses who have spent the daylight yawning as they ply their needles and, come evening, like children let out of school, are happy to put on their hats and leave in a hurry to enjoy their leisure pursuits. But that is a matter of fact, prosaic pleasure, while the twilight portends loftier and poetic pleasures.

"Blessed be the gathering dusk!" said Pushkin.* Isn't that the time of a tender, wistful sadness – not that coarse, unwelcome gloom ushered in by the daylight to everyone alike in sorrowing tears provoked by such trivial things as desperate poverty, the loss of relatives, loved ones and that kind of thing: sadness brought on by the indifference of a loved one, or because she is far away from you, or because of the obstacles which prevent you from meeting her, or by jealousy. Or could it be, and I blush to say this, that this is a time for a sweet whisper, a stammered declaration, a holding of hands and a lot of other things? And how many hopes of happiness in store and nervous expectations are cloaked under the cover of darkness! And all those preparations made for the evening's arrival! Oh how I love dusk, especially when my thoughts turn to the past! Where has that golden time gone? Will it come back... ever? Take a look at the street in twilight – it's a struggle between light and darkness; sometimes snow intervenes, brightening the scene with its own whiteness and darkening it with its cloudiness. But we humans remain idle spectators of this tussle: it abates and calls a halt – everything is still; the street is empty: the houses are like giants shrouded in the murk; no lights anywhere, and all objects merge into a single indeterminate colour; nothing interrupts the silence – not a single carriage rumbles along the road: only sleighs continue stealing silently on their way, leaving nothing but their tracks behind them on the Nevsky Prospekt. In a word, it is as if a minute of caution has ensued, although in fact it may well have been the most careless of the whole day. In winter, at twilight, an important event (for some people the most important event) takes place: dinner. For some it's a matter of eating their fill, and for others of stuffing themselves and overheating their heads with superfluous steam: just imagine the combined effect of these two factors!

Now let's enter any house at random. The whole household are gathered in the drawing room; all is quiet and no one is stirring; the conversation starts haltingly and gradually gathers momentum, skipping idly from one subject to another, and there are constant interruptions. Now take a look at their faces – it's the best time to study the true character of people and their spontaneous conversation. Look closely and you will see how at twilight their eyes reflect what's going on in their heads as they look around at ease. At one moment they are heated, the next moment contemptuous, and a moment later still they're enjoying a joke. It's then that a subordinate feels bold enough to look a superior up and down;

someone in love freely devours the loved one with his eyes and plucks up his courage to make a declaration; a con man explains in a whisper, but without grimaces, how much he's expecting to get as a kickback on a deal (that's honour among thieves for you) – and so much loose talk!... But now they're bringing in the candles, and suddenly everyone livens up. The men stand up straighter, the ladies start titivating themselves, and the conversation, which had been petering out like a stream studded with stones, comes to life like a babbling brook. And what change in the demeanour of the people! Subordinates are now peering at the polished boots of their superiors; the lover boldly approaches the table of the beloved; the crook bows and scrapes and starts ingratiating himself with the other guests with "How nice to meet you! I'm so grateful..." and "Not at all, it's the least I could do!" The incautious now regret their confidences, and look around them more discreetly. The earlier contemptuousness has now given way to a studious respectfulness and restraint. Oh, to be an observer at twilight!... But, I am told, twilight is an awkward time to be observing – it's too dark! "Yes, you are quite right!" "How did you come to forget that? Did you just forget?" "No, I just wasn't thinking."

So once in the winter at twilight in the circumstances described above, when snow was falling and the streets were silent, a frisky grey trotter, as if it had suddenly broken free of its chain, suddenly appeared either from Sadovaya or Karavannaya Street, harnessed to a small sledge in which a young man was sitting. The noble creature stretched its slender limbs, and with a proud toss of its head sped through the street, but its passenger was not satisfied.

"Get a move on!" he shouted to the driver, who, stretching out his arms as far as he had slackened his reins, stood up and urged on his steed, but to no avail. "Faster!" cried his passenger, but it was impossible to go any faster: even as it was, pedestrians were crossing the street as if they were fording a stream, and, responding to the shouts of the driver, took fright and started walking backwards, spitting in their annoyance and cursing the driver.

"He's a madman and out of his mind – he scared the hell out of us!"

The driver turned from the Nevsky Prospekt into Morskaya Street and stopped a minute later in front of a two-storey house whose aristocratic frontage included a balcony and a large porch. The young man entered with the sledge. There was no light visible in the house: it was dark everywhere even at the entrance. A doorman was seated in front of a huge stove and poking it occasionally while softly singing a sad song. At his side was a long staircase with gilded handrails.

"Is there anyone at home?" the young man asked.

"I think so," replied the doorman. "I'll call and check."

"Don't bother!" said the young man, and rushed headlong up the stairs. In the doorway it was even darker. From the corner where it was pitch-dark came the sound of snoring – the servants were asleep, relaxing before the furious activity which awaited them that evening. The young man found himself facing three doorways, unsure which one he should try to open.

"I'll just trust my instinct – it won't let me down... it will guide me to the right one," he thought, and chose to open the middle one. He passed through the long hallway and found himself in a corridor leading to a short staircase of four steps. He went up. On tiptoe and with a rapidly beating heart he went through a hallway, and, cold and feverish, entered a room. There, on a small marble table was a dimly lit lamp which revealed the faces of two old men sitting opposite each other in Voltaire armchairs, no doubt with the intention of having a chat which had eventually resolved itself into a very pleasant nap.

Anyone, not just the young man, who had been expecting to see a pair of ardent black eyes, would have been chilled by the sight of one of the sleeping old men. Imagine an enormous bald patch flanked on both sides by an upright clump of sparse hair which resembled nothing so much as a charred bush. The bald patch was followed by a nose of conical shape and considerable size towering over the upper lip, while the lower lip, with nothing barring its way, protruded a considerable distance and left the mouth wide open. At the sides of the nose and mouth there ran two deep wrinkles which disappeared among the sagging bags under the eyes. Furthermore, the entire face was wreathed in intricate arabesques. This person was none other than senior privy counsellor Baron Karl Osipovich Neyleyn, the owner of the house. I don't know who the other old man was – probably a friend of the baron; his face, however, was a great deal more decorative. Both were enjoying the sleep of the just, although the face of the first could well have been that of the most hardened criminal.

"Come on, now! Trust your heart and follow it where it leads you!" the young man reproached himself, and, turning back, he entered a small sitting room. Snoozing there on a luxurious ottoman with one leg tucked under her and the other swinging loose and her head lolling was the baron's wife. At her feet was a pug dog, which started growling immediately the young man appeared. Unwilling to cause any alarm, he hurriedly retreated.

"What happened? Where is Yelena?" he wondered, and stopped where he was, not knowing where to turn. "They're all sitting in pairs here. I'd better find her in a hurry so that we can also form a pair." At that very moment, someone played a chord on the piano in a neighbouring room, and the young man rushed in as if in response to a summons.

However, it's time to mention whom it is I am talking about and explain what he is doing in a strange house at this time of day, why he is so uninhibitedly walking about and what he is looking for. His name is Yegor Petrovich, and he is a member of the famous Aduyev family. He is a distant relative of Baron Neyleyn, and has entered his house for two reasons: one of them ordinary and the other less so – the first being kinship, as I have indicated, the other being the fact that he is in love with the delightful eighteen-year-old Yelena, the baron's daughter. She is sweet, slim and has auburn hair, and it is her that he has been looking for in the dark.

He had already declared to her parents his intention of marrying her, and they had intimated to him their approval of such a union, because Aduyev (although of course they wouldn't dream of mentioning this to him) possessed three thousand serfs as well as some other extremely satisfactory assets as a suitor and husband apart from his good looks – a factor, I would add in passing, of the greatest importance to Yelena. This mutual satisfaction was made abundantly clear by the two young people.

For all this, Yegor Petrovich sometimes complained that he was not nearly as lucky in love as he would have wished. He himself was passionately in love with all the fervour of his ardent heart, and even thought that his love for Yelena was the final reckoning with youth. His heart, weary of a series of casual loveless affairs and hardened by betrayals, was finally, after so many fruitless efforts, mustering one last effort and bringing to bear every ounce of his energy, and was now launched into a desperate struggle, from the failure of which, it seemed to him, he would emerge defeated and destroyed and no longer able to enjoy the thrill of that delightful sensation. What would life have left to offer him after such an irretrievable loss? Loving Yelena and being loved by her in return were circumstances in which life seemed to him like a garden in full bloom, and his love for Yelena seemed like a grove of luxuriant trees and a bed of brilliant flowers growing in the same plot. Without that, life seemed to him empty – an untilled field without greenery or flowers...

Aduyev's complaint was not without foundation: Yelena responded to his love with scant attention, tormented him with whims and caprices entirely in keeping with those of an Asiatic despot – and, what is more... but I'll reserve that for later and deal with it separately on another occasion. Furthermore, she permitted herself such misbehaviour only once she was confident of the commitment of Aduyev's love for her and once she was sure that there would be no turning back – that he was stranded between two extremes: suffering and bliss. Was this intolerable? I'll leave you to judge, mesdames.

After all this, what more could be expected of him? Why degrade yourself with a passion which no one will understand and for which no one will have any sympathy? Why? Don't be ridiculous! Go and ask people in love. Sheer blindness – that's all there is to it: how can it be justified? Only such people are capable of consoling themselves in a situation where those of a different disposition would be desperate – although on the other hand it could be the reverse. It sometimes seemed, for example, to Yegor Petrovich (and it may indeed have been true) that when Yelena found herself looking at him it sparked a great flame, which then resolved itself into a tender lassitude, and her cheeks grew flushed. At times she would rest her charming little head on her shoulder and with a rueful smile she found her tongue running away with her and unleashing passionate and unbridled verbal outbursts on the surface entirely out of keeping with her albeit capricious and self-indulgent behaviour, but deep down somehow consistent with her pure, demure and innocent character. Subsequently, however, when she had come to recognize the depth of his attachment, she saw that even with his enraptured language he was unable to express half of the feelings which seethed within himself. Yegor Petrovich derived some consolation from his knowledge of this, but unfortunately he also saw that she was equally attentive to the mysterious whisperings of the courtier Prince Karatyzhkin, and that her eyes lingered just as long on the colourful uniform of the cavalry officer Zbruyev, the only difference being that they did not leave her wondering for a minute – and sometimes their three voices joined in harmonious laughter. He couldn't stand the sight of that hateful trio, and he always made a swift exit with an aching heart.

All this sometimes drove Aduyev to distraction. "Why does she give me such tender looks?" he wondered. "Why?" Afterwards he supplied himself silently with the answer. "Because she's in love – of course, that's it! She said so herself." Then, other questions occurred to him. "But why does she cast such lingering looks at Prince Karatyzhkin and Zbruyev? Why is she always smiling at them and never annoyed with them – the way she is with me? And what is that whispering all about?" These were questions to which he could find no answer, and this enraged him.

And indeed what word could you use to describe Yelena's behaviour? Aduyev, beside himself with anger, found a word – but please, mesdames, I'm talking about Aduyev and not myself! Well, what should I call it? My memory's like a sieve! It's such a bizarre un-Russian word... it's on the tip of my tongue. I've got it! Coquetry! Coquetry! I finally got it! This is the way I see it, mesdames: it's a virtue of your fair sex... to surround yourselves with an entourage of idle young men and, out of compassion for their inactivity, find something for them to do. It was, as it was put by Aduyev himself (he was bilious at times), a club whose members commit to endearing themselves to a chosen woman: the membership fee takes the form of work, running errands and fussing over them; their reward is tentative, sensitive and fiery and passionate glances, all feigned of course, and artificial, but no less well meant than the real thing. Some are rewarded with affectionate taps on the nose with a fan, a hand offered to be kissed, a dance or two in the evening, and permission to call outside visiting times – but to reap this reward what is required is extraordinary zeal and perseverance.

To run from Yelena, to get away from his love and pay the price of being scorned, as I have already said, was beyond Yegor Petrovich. Furthermore, there still lurked within him a spark of hope for happiness. He had been studying her character in the expectation that she would finally lose interest in all that hustle and bustle, and ultimately tire of those barren triumphs of self-esteem, which would give way to a feeling of true love within her, perhaps even stronger than before. It was for this reason alone that he kept refraining from asking for her hand.

Fearful that he might be encountering some new caprice and hopeful of finding Yelena alone, he entered the room where the piano was being played, but unfortunately Yelena was in the company of a ginger-haired Englishwoman, who was sitting beside her knitting a scarf with very long bone needles. Very soon, however, the duenna was called away and did not return. What luck! He was left alone with her.

Yelena Karlovna was a nice and pleasant young woman, and Yegor was nice and pleasant too. Is it any wonder that fate has thrown them together in a small room? Surely not the old baron and his wife! Out of the question! They themselves felt uneasy about the impropriety of the situation and made a point of not sitting too close together. If they ever did, it would be only at dinner among other guests and as a sensible and respectable married couple.

Yelena barely glanced at Aduyev, and, hardly acknowledging his gracious bow, continued playing the piano somewhat louder and faster than before in order to give the impression that she was totally absorbed in her playing. He looked at her with delight and in silence.

"Why didn't you go to see Papa instead of coming straight to me?" she asked flatly.

"Yelena!" Yegor Petrovich responded in a voice in which there was a hint of reproach.

"Mademoiselle Helène or Yelena Karlovna, if you don't mind! You're becoming too familiar: soon you'll be calling me Alenushka."

"He... lè... ne!" The young man pronounced the word with trepidation in his heart and his voice.

"Yegor Petrovich," she responded coolly, but with an edge of tenderness, unwittingly mimicking Aduyev's voice and look.

"So?" He uttered the syllable mournfully after a long silence.

"So!" she repeated teasingly, pounding a chord on the piano.

"You're teasing me, Yelena Karlovna."

"Not at all! I'm just trying to respond in the same spirit and tone as you in order to please you. How more attentive could I possibly be?"

"If I weren't so sure that you are just joking, I would—"

"What would you—"

"I would have left the room long ago."

"Well, that's something new!" Yelena remarked caustically. "I've never heard that before. But in any case, what's rubbing you up the wrong way? I'm always pleased to see you. I'm sure you can tell this from the look in my eyes. I'm more considerate to you than I am to others. With them I just try to be amiable and civil."

"So, it's just a matter of civility! One can't try to be amiable, baroness, it's not something that can be acquired. If someone is nice to you, he is not trying to be nice. In any case, true kindness has its limits, and your relations with Prince Karatyzhkin and Zbruyev…"

"So that's it! You don't like my relationship with them… I wonder why. As a matter of fact, you should welcome the attention they pay me, which is a tribute to my personality, as they say themselves."

"Oh yes, listen to them!"

"What do you mean? It's nothing but the truth. And I believe you share their opinion – or at least that's what I deduce from your love."

Aduyev bit his lip.

"But your coldness and the strange way you're treating me… it's getting unbearable!" he said.

"Then don't bear it."

"Then tell me with the same sincerity I no longer see in you: do you love me?"

"This is so boring! You go on and on! You've long known the answer."

"But since then a lot might have changed – and has done!" he sighed.

She sighed in her turn.

"Baroness, no one has ever thought of me as a fool or a child. Your ridicule is the first I've ever experienced. Another five minutes of this… and I'll…"

"And you'll what?"

"I'll leave you this minute – and for good!"

"How terrifying!"

Aduyev's patience had been tested by Yelena's mockery, and he lost his temper.

"Very well! I'm leaving, and I'll do my best to forget this impossible woman before whom I've been grovelling so fruitlessly!" Yegor Petrovich burst out. "My God! Can this be the woman I have revered and in whose finer feelings I so blindly believed, and whose love I never thought myself worthy of winning? Look at her! Hardly had she pronounced the words 'I love you' for the first time in her life than she had already forgotten how sacred were those pledges and commitments, giving priority to empty formalities!"

"What commitments? It's not as if we were engaged, you know?"

"But how can I ask for your hand when you behave like this with me and others, and are still unsure of your feelings? As headstrong and capricious as you are, how can I face the future with any confidence? Why are you silent?"

She clasped her hands together, lowered her eyes and bowed her head.

"I await your orders," she said.

"So you've decided to insult me! Goodbye, baroness!" He picked up his hat.

"But where are you going? Don't you want to stay for tea with us?" she said provocatively. "Mama and Papa would be so pleased to see you..."

Aduyev remained silent for a few moments.

"Thank you!" he said, breaking the silence. "You have opened my eyes. I came here to put my cards on the table and to find out what was in your heart, something which has long been a mystery and a puzzle for me. I wanted to know whether it still belonged to me, and I needed you to explain your treatment of me – whether you were simply being frivolous. I intended to propose to you in the hope that once you had accepted the obligations of marriage you would no longer be so whimsical and capricious. But now, after this conversation, I need no more explanations. It's clear that I have nothing more to hope for: you don't love me!"

"So that's what you think?"

"You can laugh if you want. But you will see that I am not a child! I was ready to devote my life to you and be your husband when I saw that we could be happy together, and felt sure that my love was reciprocated – but to take you to the altar without love, coldly, for the sake of respectability and fulfilling other people's expectations – this is impossible for me, and you are now free to renege on your word!"

"Fine words indeed!"

Aduyev paid no attention to what she had said and continued.

"I confess that up until now I lived only for your love, and my dearest wish was for your love. Don't think, however, that I would have placed my trust as lightly in an experienced woman. Oh no! Your youth, and the feelings you revealed to me at the beginning, gave me every reason to believe in the unblemished purity and sincerity of your heart. Who could have suspected then—"

"Suspected what?"

"All that evasiveness, pretence and coquetry…"

"You are forgetting yourself, Monsieur Aduyev!" she rebuked him haughtily.

"Is this the way you were before? And right now, when my head is teeming with those memories, my eyes are brimming with tears… In spite of your icy coldness and your contempt, I would forgive you even that for the sake of the past, if I could detect a tiny remnant of that feeling. No, I repeat, I'm not a child, and I know that there is not a glimmer of hope: that has been swept away, just as everything else is eventually!"

Aduyev fell silent. Yelena glanced at her watch.

"Surely you remember," he began again, "who it was who kindled the flames of that fire. How did you learn such guile? Young as you are, how did such treachery insinuate itself in your heart – a heart which had seemed to breathe nothing but sincerity and wholeheartedness? When I returned from abroad weary and out of sorts and depressed and seeking only solitude, who was it who greeted me with a welcoming smile, radiating the promise of a future which, I now see, was never to materialize? It was you, Yelena, with your enchanting smile, who brought me back to life, ready to meet its myriad challenges, some of which you yourself were facing, and in which I hastened to join you..."

Yelena yawned.

"Don't you remember, when we sat together for hours in this very place or in the garden of the dacha, forgetting the world and wanting to see nobody but me? When I was wasting away like a withering plant, wasn't it you, like a guardian angel, who told me to 'live for love'?"

"I don't believe I said that."

"It was then that you somehow solved for me the problem of how to be happy. I greedily absorbed those reassuring words and began to see things through your eyes – eyes in which there shone a warm light not only of empathy, but also partnership and loving commitment, which seemed to be telling me: 'Love me, and a whole new world of bliss will open up – I will not only create your happiness, but share it with you.' Don't you remember?"

"How can you rake up that old nonsense? It was so long ago! Do you really still remember all that?"

"I closed my eyes. 'So much for happiness!' I thought. I was chasing an illusion – and had landed in an abyss. But how I loved you... how much! Now I'm ashamed to admit that to myself. It was the last thing that my heart had to give, the last dying echo of my feeling – and it is all this that you are destroying so ruthlessly!"

Yelena was casually playing with a lock of her hair and apparently looking at a picture on the wall, but if someone had been scrutinizing the expression which came and went in her eyes, that someone would have wagged his finger at her to let her know that he knew it was all an act.

"What an inexplicable change!" Aduyev put in. "Coldness, ridicule, caprice – is this how you expected to teach me to love life? Is this the reward for my devotion? On whom you are lavishing all your attentions and all your tenderness? And to what end? To become a subject of malicious gossip among riff-raff? So that your precious name, so cherished by me, can be bandied about among scoundrels? So that your actions can be seen in a dubious light? Maybe in time you will come to remember me and sigh not in mockery, not ironically, but from your heart – even when you're married. Goodbye, Yelena Karlovna! That's all I have to say."

"That's all? Thank God! I think you must be tired?"

"I will not humiliate myself any further. I can only thank God that I stopped in time."

He gave her a sketchy bow, and she stood up and made a gracious and ceremonial curtsy.

"It pains me to see how much your heart has been hardened by the life you've been living. This is a bitter moment for me: instead of reaching out your hand to me in a gesture of sympathy and consolation, or even giving me a friendly look rather than one of bliss (that bliss which you so casually promised but have proved unable to deliver), you have nothing to offer me but your scathing indifference! You have no idea what deep wounds you have inflicted on what was already a heart in agony. This is the last time you will ever see me in your home!"

"But why do you wish to deprive us of the pleasure of your company? We are at home on Tuesdays and Fridays. I hope you won't refuse to be among our guests and…"

Aduyev had stopped listening and hurried out of the room in despair.

But what about her? She continued playing random chords on the piano as the sound of his footsteps died away, and when they could no longer be heard, she covered her face with her hands and burst into tears. That proud Yelena, the aristocrat, that shrew, was sobbing her heart out? It doesn't make sense! When only a minute before with such cold indifference – even ridicule – she dismissed a man passionately in love and devoted to her? I ask you, how can anyone make sense of that? What was going on in her mind at the time – and afterwards? What devil possessed her to respond with sarcasm to Aduyev's declaration? And what angel was now making her cry? Why, proud beauty that you are, didn't you cry a minute earlier? Don't you know, inexperienced child that you are, that a single tear shed by you would have pierced that young man's heart, and that, overcome with guilt, he would have fallen at your feet? A single tear of yours would have provoked an eloquent outburst, testifying to the intensity of his devotion. But your pride inhibited you. You missed your opportunity – he wasn't here to witness your tears. Instead of an ecstatic shudder of love, his heart was pierced by a cold dagger and wrenched with grief. Now his only impulse is to flee as far away as possible in order to swallow his rejection and drown it with new impressions. Just think of it! A single tear of yours would only have redoubled his devotion and made him your slave. You could at least have pretended. But it's too late now!

However, if you set aside her pride, which prevented Yelena from acting straightforwardly instead of behaving capriciously and trying to have her way – as is usual for pretty girls – is Yelena really to blame?

She is a spirited young woman, intelligent and well educated, good-hearted and well meaning. Her need to stand up to Yegor Petrovich was the product of her upbringing. She bore the hallmarks of the school from which she graduated and the circle in which she had been raised from childhood.

When she was still in her infancy, she noticed that even her own mother regarded her devoted spouse in the normal way that most people regard one another, although regarding young people rather differently from the norm. She began to understand that there were differences between the two sexes. For instance, she saw Princess Z— talking to Colonel A— about the weather, the theatre or even military manoeuvres in the company of others. When they were seated at some distance from other people, the conversation tended to be different: it became more animated, as did their facial expressions – but when others were nearby, voices were lowered. From this she concluded that even casual conversation was of two kinds. When she grew up, however, she became more observant, although her expression and conversation remained the same whether she was talking to someone in the company of others or alone. She saw that Countess R—'s box was always crowded with young men, and when she was about to leave, those same young men were almost competing for the right to hand her her coat. On the other hand, when she was at a ball... well, at a ball she was unapproached! What could all this mean? Our beauty pondered long and hard. "You're very nice," the countess in question finally explained to her, "but you don't have what it takes to attract those young men. You're too inaccessible. There's something cold about you. One look from you and a crowd of even the nicest young men would disperse. See what an interest Ladov is taking in you, and how warmly Surkov greets you – he's always hanging around in your vicinity. When they crowd around you, all you do is blush like a schoolgirl and respond like a priest's wife."

"A priest's wife! How awful!" Yelena groaned. "Just you wait, countess! There's going to be a lot more room in your box!" I don't know what the countess may have said to her after that, but the very next day after that lesson Yelena found herself in the company of her cousin, a cadet in a guards regiment, and at the first ball after the conversation she found herself exhausted from a surfeit of admirers.

From that day forth, Yelena was confident of the charm she possessed and understood its power. She had created a magic spell around herself, drawing on those resources with which she had been endowed by nature and her upbringing: maidenly innocence and moral purity. Wielding her charm was nothing more than a diversion for her – but it was very useful in her social life. She was not modelling herself entirely on one of those countesses.

But what about her heart?

It had long remained cold and inert, and started beating only when Aduyev came on the scene – and then started to beat fast and often. Yelena yielded willingly to the effects of this glorious and novel feeling. For about a month and a half she stopped being a brilliant debutante and went back to being the old enchanting

Yelena with all that unfeigned and simple charm. For a time she became totally immersed in herself, and discovered the treasures with which she had been endowed by nature. She picked Aduyev from among the throng of suitors for his intelligence, his innate nobility and strength of character and will, but most importantly her feminine instinct told her the kind of passionate feeling he was capable of: he alone was the kind of man who could make her happy, the only one she could ever love the way she did, because he alone conformed to the ideal, the embodiment of which she had been seeking in vain from among those society suitors. She had figured all this out for herself... after all, young women can think – and even calculate – for themselves! So having worked all this out and having fallen for him head over heels, she began to beguile him – not with those charms which had proved so effective with others: she won his love by revealing the treasures of her mind, heart and soul. Captivated as he was, and confident of happiness, he was carried away by the prospect of an idyllic future and surrendered himself heart and soul to the enchantress. Confident that her feelings were returned and that their love was mutual, but above all sure of their future happiness, Yelena found no reason not to revert to her old habits, which in her view were no impediment to love, and which it would have been difficult for her to give up, because otherwise all those social butterflies would keep their distance, and also because it would have been detrimental in the eyes of society to her amiable reputation and perhaps (it's only human nature) even sow doubts about her beauty, demeaning her in the eyes of her competitors and knocking her off her perch as the belle of the ball. And God knows what other troubles might have followed! There's no way that only one man will find her attractive! Impossible! She is right, but I'll leave it up to my readers of the fair sex to be the judges.

In that case, is Yegor Petrovich to blame? No, he cannot be found guilty either. He was born under a different star, which early on removed him from high society and steered him in another direction, although he had been born into that same circle.

His well-intentioned and intelligent parents, mindful as they were of both his material and moral development, gave him an excellent education, and on his graduation from the university sent him abroad and then died. The young man benefited greatly from his travels both intellectually and emotionally, met many people and developed a broad-minded view of things, travelling widely in Europe and accumulating experiences of every kind – not all of them pleasant, and leaving him wary of people and with an ironic view of life. He lost his belief in happiness, ceased to expect any joy from it and endured stoically the fate meted out to him. He cultivated a kind of "woe from wit"* attitude. Someone else in his position and with his means would have been delighted... leading a quiet life, strolling on the Nevsky Prospekt and reading the "Reading Library". But he found his quiet, trouble-free and uneventful life unsatisfying and arid – an existence that to him was nothing but an unending sleep. He felt that he was simply vegetating – not living a life. What a crank!

When he thought of Yelena, he appreciated how important she was to him and how happy he would be if he won her love – a happiness that would last his whole life. He snapped out of his trance and summoned life from the depths of his soul, armed himself with the merits and virtues he knew he possessed and went into battle for the young woman's heart. He was successful, jubilant and proud that his feelings were powerful enough to prevail regardless of her dominant weaknesses, because, as we have seen, she had temporarily overcome them.

He had formed a distinct idea of her, and, trembling with love, was in thrall to her virtues, confident of the unalloyed happiness that lay before him, confident that there was a light at the end of the tunnel, that there was a state which he might call happiness. "Yes, now I'm beginning to live!" he told himself. Suddenly he had a vision of this happiness as unalloyed and untrammelled, elevated by the promptings and nobility of the soul above the madding crowd of the young. He was never one to lavish flattery on women or to go out of his way to attract their momentary attention, and was too experienced to give way to deception or to succumb to the rewards which were so avidly sought after by others.

He avoided (he couldn't bring himself to utter the word) coquettes, although it's important to call things by their proper names. He had a very definite idea of the kind of woman he was ready to call his own – perhaps an old-fashioned, romantic, barbaric notion. Loving as he did so passionately and so strongly, he thought a woman should devote herself to him alone body and soul just as he did to her, and not lavish attention or affection on others, but sacrifice them as precious offerings on the altar of love. She should know no pleasure unconnected with him and should share his grief and all his feelings. Should he be blamed then in the light of the foregoing for being displeased with Yelena's behaviour? "Sheer barbarity!" my readers of the fair sex may say. But I'll leave that up to the judgement of my readers.

So who is to blame? In my view, no one. If their fate depended on me, I would dispense with them here and now and end my story. But let us see what happens next.

They parted – perhaps even for ever. Her pride prevented Yelena from revealing her true feelings. Right now she is shedding tears, quite probably having decided to make a sacrifice for the sake of love if only he would return – something which was her greatest wish and upon which her happiness depended. It was only then that she realized how much he meant to her and how much she loved him. But he is not coming back. A terrible feeling has taken root in him, a feeling that drives out love – the pride, the arrogance of a man long languishing in passion and finally rejected. He had freed himself from the chains of his fruitless enslavement, raised his head proudly, and was singing a hymn of freedom... Poor Yelena! But enough – is this the way it was? We shall see.

Twilight had faded into darkness. The lights were on in the rooms, people were bustling about. Conversation could be heard in the baron's study; the old men had called for seltzer water, and conversation went on, interrupted only by sleep. In the room of the baron's wife a bell had been rung; there was movement everywhere; the evening had begun, but Yelena was still sitting motionless in the same place with her head lowered. Although her tears had given way to a pallor, the expression in her eyes was just short of despair. She was no longer that belle of the ball, her head held high, surrounded by a throng of admirers ready to do her bidding, always demure, always majestic, with a haughty look and a triumphant smile. No, the tinsel was gone. Her grief had knocked her off her pedestal, and no one who saw her in this condition would have taken her to be the glamorous star of the highest society: everyone would have said that this was just an unhappy young woman.

You might say that her unhappiness is imaginary and does not warrant sympathy – that there is no real reason for it. The way I see it is that, regardless of the reason, if someone is suffering, then that person must be unhappy. Is it caused by a nervous disorder? It is still suffering, and it doesn't matter if it's imaginary or the result of an actual loss. There is no universal yardstick for measuring unhappiness. Misfortune can only be judged in terms of the person suffering it and not in relation to others. You must put yourself in that person's place and see it from their perspective.

Well, yes, Yelena was unhappy, and moreover it was not imaginary. Yelena's love for Aduyev was not a transitory thing: she too was deeply in love, and it was heartfelt. It was her first and perhaps her last love. Her intelligence and depth of feeling superseded by far that of those around her. Having spent her day at the festival of vanity, having satisfied her ego and collected a plentiful tribute of adoration for her beauty and courtesy, what was on her mind when she was alone that evening? She thought about how happy she was to be loved, about her future life, which she was resolved to spend with Aduyev. The social whirl had not filled the void in her heart: vanity had infiltrated her soul by mistake. She herself was impatiently awaiting her marriage, when she would belong to one man alone. And suddenly all hope had been lost! He no longer loved her and had lost all his respect for her. It was sheer torture! With the young man out of her life, the future was wrapped in a mournful shroud. She would be alone for ever. Robbed of her heart's desire, she was left at the mercy of fate. God knows who she would end up marrying; she might find herself a victim of the diplomatic machinations of her father. Right now she found herself disgusted by the attentions of all those suitors.

Yes, she was truly unhappy, and failed to hear the door open to admit a red-haired Englishwoman: she only learnt of her arrival when she babbled something inarticulate about the hairdresser waiting for her in the dressing room and that Mama had told her to remind her about the ball.

The ball! Oh God, that was all she needed! "I'm not going to the ball, you hear?" she replied in English. "Tell Mama, tell the hairdresser, tell everyone that I can't, I won't!" She spoke like someone at the end of her tether, and if she had been a man, she would probably have added "Goddammit!"

However, it was out of the question not to go to the ball. She would have to feign sickness for at least a couple of weeks... what would people say? So, like a lamb to the slaughter, she was marched into the dressing room with her dresser.

And what a dressing room! What luxury! Such good taste! I've seen such things before in Gumbs, Junker and Plincke,* but they never made such an impression on me. It's because every single item perfectly matches all the others – it's because they appear in the temple of a goddess and each one bears the stamp of her presence and seems to have a life of its own. For instance, what is so special about this bronze candlestick with a lampshade if you see it in a shop window? But when you see only the stub of the burnt-down candle next to the open book and the initialled handkerchief of our beauty and imagine her seated at the book and reading, the whole scene takes on a magical charm, even if the book is nothing more than, say, the *Works* of Figlyarin* (which, it so happens, Yelena, God bless her soul, has never read). But what's so special about this scene? Nothing but a dressing table with a mirror! Ah, but on it there rests her glove turned inside out, tiny, scented with amber. It's impossible to imagine that it's the scent of a French perfume – it has to be that of the little hand that wears it. There's a divan along with the rest of the exquisite furniture. But our beauty used it to change her shoes, and on it is a tiny shoe left behind by the chambermaid. How carelessly the ribbons have been hung! It's so adorable! You look around to see if anyone is there – in particular Aduyev. You clutch the treasure in your hand and kiss it – you can't resist!

Now Yelena is seated in an armchair facing a mirror, barely aware of what is happening around her, although she is being fussed over by a hairdresser and three chambermaids. At this moment she feels radiant – much better even than at one of those receptions where she comes equipped with an armoury of special gestures, glances and words. She is now a prey to her grief – and looking much the better for it! How can she not understand that she is at her best when she is in the grip of an overpowering and genuine feeling? She is sitting at her ease, and for once not looking at herself in the mirror. Her ever-lively, mobile eyes are darkened and clouded by a gloomy reverie, and tears are glistening in her eyes; on her cheeks the rosy glow is effaced by an intermittent pallor; her lips are parted, and her head is lowered to her left shoulder. She is oblivious to the fact that one of the pins in her coiffure has come loose and that the hairs of her lustrous curls are dangling against her cheek and upon her shoulder. She has not noticed that the chambermaids, in their attempts to put on her dancing shoes, have taken off those she had been wearing and provided a velvet cushion on which she can rest her charming, dainty foot.

I've now come to understand why it is that you never find a hairdresser with a pensive or gloomy disposition, and why they're always cheerful and talkative – and why it couldn't be otherwise. No matter how morose they may be by nature, the very fact that they touch the heads of attractive young women with their fingers must have a magical effect. Elegance acts on even the most insensitive characters, especially when it takes the form of

Yelena's head. How brusquely the hairdresser takes possession of Yelena's pretty little head! He pushes it up and he pushes it down, turns it to the right and turns it to the left, with all the deftness of an expert. How freely he runs his fingers back and forth along her scalp! One minute he is bending down as if to breathe in her fragrance, and the next minute he is leaning back as if to admire her scalp from afar in the same way that an artist surveys his work; see how he has grasped an entire lock of hair with one hand, while with the other... What delights are revealed with every movement! No, your patience is exhausted! You may be looking at an ivory crucifix on the small table, you may be thinking pious thoughts to contain your feelings, but nothing helps! Your head is hot, your eyes are dimmed, your blood is ebbing and flowing rapidly in your heart. You try to avert your gaze, only to encounter a new temptation! Spread out on the divan in captivating disorder is a gauzy garment which at any moment will be enclosing our beauty, girding, embracing and outlining her voluptuous figure – her dress is so light, airy and ethereal that if you and I together, my dear reader, were to blow on it, it would flutter away!

No! I will never again venture into such places. I would be better advised to take a look at what Yegor Petrovich is up to. He is descending the stairs not nearly as cheerfully as he climbed them. It seems as if he is stopping on each stair to reflect. His legs are giving way as if, to use Victor Hugo's expression, he had two knees on each leg.*

After leaving the house where he had been so cruelly offended, and to which he had no intention of ever returning, he just felt like shaking off the dust from his feet,* but he probably simply forgot to do so and just made his way quietly along the street, after telling the coachman to follow him. What a difference between his arrival and his departure! For an hour he still had had every hope of convincing Yelena and winning her heart and her hand, and now she no longer existed for him. He walked slowly, the way all disheartened people do, his head hanging, his eyes on the ground in front of him, hearing and feeling nothing. Finally he arrived home. If his servant hadn't relieved him of his coat almost forcibly, he would have kept it after entering the house. As it was, with his hat still on his head, he plumped himself down in a place where he had never sat before and started muttering to himself: "Such is life! Only an hour ago I could still call myself happy, but now!... What a fool! What a child! My experience has taught me nothing. I was confident of happiness. What good did it do me that I knew life inside out and that I had witnessed so many others stumbling at every step and yet continuing to fall victim to the same old deception? I fell into the trap with my eyes open! I'm so ashamed of myself! But who could have resisted her charms? In any case, I wasn't so happy... I stood firm for a long time... but I'm only human! It was my last hope, and the disappointment is all the more painful for that. It's sheer misery to have seen my dearest dream shattered."

He remained plunged in thought for a long time, and finally stood up and started walking fast around the room.

"Where to begin? How can I cope with my misery?" He was lost in thought. Finally a totally different expression appeared in his eyes. He was livid with anger, and his lips were clenched. "No!" he exclaimed. "I will not give way to my grief. I refuse to languish under this burden! My honour is at stake! No! I am strong enough to give up this unattainable dream – and forget about it. I have what it takes to assert myself! Reading or the studies I have abandoned will not be of any help. I'll take up travelling – all over the world! I'll go to Germany and learn new things! I'll live under the blessed skies of Italy and Greece. They say that travel is the panacea for those stricken with this folly. God knows, I have so much to do! For instance, for a whole month I haven't seen my estate manager and have no idea what's going on in my villages – after all, I am responsible for three thousand lives and their welfare. No time to waste! I'll get right down to it. Oh yes! I will recover my lost tranquillity – after all, I am a man!"

"Hey," he cried, and a servant appeared. "Send the estate manager to my study right away!"

Five minutes later, Yegor Petrovich's manager entered his study carrying a sheaf of papers. He was short and completely bald, and wore a pea-green morning coat. He made a low bow and waited at the door.

"We haven't seen each other for a long time, Yakov! How is it that you don't come and see me on business?"

"I do come, Yegor Petrovich, sir. Every day, as I've always done, but I'm always told that you have gone to see Baron Karl Osipovich."

"Well, today was the last time! From now on they won't be saying that any more, and I will be watching and overseeing everything"

"Yes, sir!" said the old man and bowed low.

"So, what do you have to report?"

"Well sir, the architect from the Voronezh estate has written to ask if you would be good enough to give a date for the completion of the house in Yeltsy. There is still quite a lot of work left to do, and the spring will soon be here. And the gardener is asking for seeds to be sent for the flower garden you have asked for. He has sent a list, but it is not written in our usual way."

"They're both lying!" said Aduyev angrily, interrupting him. "None of that is needed. Stop the construction and dismiss the architect. And forget that business for the garden! I won't be going there."

"Yes, sir!" said the old man, and made a low bow.

Aduyev had every reason to be angry. All his private plans for improving his country house and his garden were an integral part of his future marriage. He had already begun to visualize Yelena as his wife, revelling in the prospect of their happiness and working out the details of its implementation. His Voronezh village was ideally situated for their life together, and as for the old, gloomy unprepossessing home of his grandfather, his idea was to make of it a glorious temple of love – it would be his El Dorado. He had made a study of Yelena's tastes down to the last detail, and was able to anticipate her wishes, which in conjunction with his own he had begun to implement in terms of changes in the country house and its garden. He had invited the architect and sent to St Petersburg for the plans for the works on the house, issuing a long list of instructions for the gardener. He had already given thought to the purchase of furniture and the decor and had mentally organized the distribution of work. He had envisaged his future family life and was mindful of the need to add to his library the works of Yelena's favourite authors. He often thought of the time when he would install the beloved new chatelaine in his grandfather's home and embark on a new stage of his life. A landowner, the benefactor of his people, a husband in possession of a charming wife and later on a father – what a glittering future! But suddenly – and who would have thought it! – he became possessed by a demonic fury when the estate manager reminded him of the plans which had now become nothing more than castles in the air and quite pointless.

Once again he started pacing the room.

"What is it now?" he asked impatiently.

"The headman of the Yaroslav estate," Yakov began nervously, "has written to ask whether Your Honour would be willing to do something to help two young lads – it's their turn to be drafted. The father of one of them broke his leg in the autumn and sits on the stove with his hands clasped. He and his son are the only breadwinners in his family – the others are all women and children. Someone else might have married off his son to an orphan – a hard-worker who would have been a treasure to any family. So much hardship, writes the headman, it makes your heart bleed to see them."

Aduyev frowned. "What's this? A bride? I'll give him a bride! He must be crazy to think of marrying! What nonsense! Send both of them to the army, and the girl to a factory! And if the headman writes again, pack him off to the same place! I'm not joking, you hear?"

"Of course! My dear Yegor Petrovich, I'll draft a reply tomorrow."

"Next!"

"Some peasants from a Kursk village have sent a petition complaining bitterly about the poor harvest. Would you mind putting off the arrears for another year?"

"Nonsense! I want to see every penny collected... or else! You understand?"

"If Your Honour so wishes, sir. I'll write tomorrow," replied the old man, and made a low bow.

"Anything else?"

"No, sir"

"You can go! And make sure that you report in full back to me!"

The estate manager left the room and entered the hall, where another old man awaited him. It was Yelisei, Aduyev's valet.

"My dear Yakov Tikhonych, what has happened to Yegor Petrovich? Can you find out? I'm at a loss – I've never seen him like this."

Yakov waved his hand and recounted what had happened between them – how the master had responded to the serfs' petition and to the request of the conscripted boys. "So like his father!" And this was how Yakov concluded his remarks. "He's only human, you know..."

"What are you saying, Yakov Tikhonych!"

"I swear it's true."

The old men offered each other tobacco and parted. Meanwhile, Aduyev had been pacing the room in an extremely worried state.

"Well, I've calmed down now!" he said, as he feverishly tugged at a button from his morning coat with one hand and scratched his ear with the other hand so hard that he almost drew blood. "Yes, I'm completely calm! Now that I've achieved that, I can move on to the next task... I'm going to put her out of my mind!"

At that very moment the Devil reminded him of the estate manager's report on the works on the country house, and his imagination brought back the vivid image of his lost happiness and that idyllic refuge – the house, its comfort, its good taste, its luxury and the delightful garden where art wrangled with nature, and where he and Yelena together would be safe from their foolish neighbours and the rest of the world. It would be there that he would lie with his magic mirror at the feet of his Armida.*

But all was lost! That magnificent edifice of his imagination had crumbled. He wrenched off the button completely and scratched his ear until it bled.

"No, it's despicable – cowardly!" he cried out. "Enough of these treacherous thoughts and seductive dreams! Don't try to comfort me! I'm going to banish you from my memory. I'm going to join a riotous gang of lecherous men. I'll sing their songs, and in the midst of their orgies I'll blot out her memory – I'll scream my heart out... Tomorrow will be the start of a new life!" He picked up a pen and a sheet of paper and began to write.

Five minutes later he called for Yelisei.

"Tomorrow I will have lunch with the twenty men who are on this list. Send out messengers with invitations. I'll leave you to make arrangements for the dinner. Make sure it's sumptuous and with plenty of champagne, and we'll be playing cards!... "

"Forgive me sir, but it's already late at night – how will you manage?"

"I'll leave that up to you! I don't want to know anything! Just make sure it happens, you old devil – no more of your fancy talk... and get out!"

The old man's first reaction was surprise, but he ended up shaking his head sadly as he looked at Aduyev.

"What the devil," he whispered, "what do you mean? You never had it so good... I never expected this from you at my age, Yegor Petrovich... I looked after you when you were a child... I served your father for thirty years and was with him in the Turkish campaign, and in all that time I never heard an unkind word from him."

Without a word Aduyev pointed at the door. The old man wiped away a tear and picked up Aduyev's list from the floor, and left with his head lowered.

"My God!" Aduyev exclaimed bitterly. "What has this passion done to me! I must be out of my mind!"

He covered his face with his handkerchief, sobbing bitterly but without shedding tears. He was a terrible and yet pitiful sight. He felt hot, and struggled to breathe – it was unbearable. His face was showing signs of his inner turmoil and physical stress, while only a couple of hours ago it was fresh, handsome and glowing with health. It had now changed beyond recognition; his eyes had lost their glitter, the way they would have after a long illness. His cheeks were sunken, his features distorted and his hair in disarray. His fury and grief finally gave way to a quiet sadness, and he became calmer, at least outwardly. One hand was lying on the table – with the other he was toying mindlessly with a ticket that was there. Eventually his glance fell on it and read: "Entrance ticket for a ball at the Commercial Club."

"Where did this ticket come from?" he asked, after summoning his servant.

"A gentleman brought it and asked me to tell you that he hoped you would attend."

"Well, it seems that Fate has provided me with some entertainment. I will go where she seems to be expecting me. Who knows? It may even surprise me and make my day!"

"Help me to get dressed!" he told his servant, and gave orders to prepare the carriage.

"Do you know where the Commercial Club is?" he asked the driver.

"No, I don't, sir."

"Somewhere on the English Embankment – you'll have to ask."

"Oh yes… now I know."

"Then take me there!"

All journalists who report on balls never forget to mention a totally banal and obvious fact: that the porch and the windows are brightly lit and the street outside is blocked by carriages. And in any case, how can a gathering of respectable people ever do without all this? Of course, to describe all these details, as Pushkin did in his *Eugene Onegin*,* is another matter! So I will refer anyone who happens to be interested in such details to that work, and I will say no more about it because I have no intention of giving a description of the ball, which I am mentioning for only one reason: namely, that it has a direct bearing on the fate of Yegor Petrovich.

Aduyev entered the building, shoved the ticket into the hand of the elaborately uniformed doorman and mounted the staircase, which was covered with a lavish carpet that would have graced many an office or study. Both sides were lined with a row of grapefruit and lemon trees. The doors bore gilded engravings and had glass windows. The hallway was teeming with waiters dressed in velvet and decorated in gold. In a word, it was entirely worthy of any aristocratic ball.

"A public ball! And yet so luxurious!" thought Aduyev. "How unusual!"

The doors opened to reveal a series of brightly lit rooms. He stood for a minute just inside the hall inspecting the crowd with his lorgnette, and was surprised to see the entire "cream" of St Petersburg's aristocracy. He was passed by a constant stream of stars, ribbons and every conceivable uniform, due to the presence of representatives from all countries. Also present were the kind of young people who would have stood out in any gathering – even at the Last Judgement, when the whole of mankind is gathered together – simply on account of their appearance. The tone, the behaviour, the clothing expressed the highest degree of elegance, perfection, simplicity and naturalness which cannot be counterfeited. Arrayed in this way were the crème de la crème of dandies, whose upbringing seemed to have been blessed by nature itself.

"But what are they all doing here?" Aduyev wondered. "I've never even heard about the 'Commercial Club'."

He found a mirror, cast a critical glance at his own attire and entered the hall.

Near the doors stood an old gentleman of respectable appearance in a foreign uniform. He exchanged bows with Aduyev and uttered some words of welcome.

"They've done all they could to make this ball different from a public one," thought Yegor Petrovich. "Some old fellow greeted me as if he were the host! Of course he must have seen me at the baron's."

He politely returned the bow and moved away. Finally, when he reached the place where the first part of the ball – the dancing – was taking place, he stopped. There were assembled the glamorous ladies (whom Aduyev does his best to avoid) who adorn the mezzanine of the Mikhailovsky Theatre in the evenings and the Nevsky Prospekt in the mornings, and decorate the balconies of country dachas in the summer. These first-magnitude stars of St Petersburg society radiate all the colours of the rainbow. What refined sophistication! What elegance and good taste in their outfits! All this respectability left him cold, just as any thinking man would be turned off by all that stuffiness. He inwardly cursed Bronsky, who had given him the ticket. "Damn him!" he growled. "Why didn't he warn me? Of course he only meant to surprise me, and I have to admit that he managed to do that very well. Anyway, where is he? Why hasn't he arrived by now?"

At that moment, one of the most glittering stars stopped to speak to him. "So you are here, Monsieur Aduyev? A rare appearance. You are so unsociable. Who brought you here?"

"It was Bronsky, princess."

"Oh, I thought it was the baron," she said, and moved away, taking with her a short little princess, like a ship towing a boat.

"Of course," thought Yegor Petrovich, moving on. "The baron will go to the Commercial Club even though Your Excellency is here. All his colleagues and fellow whist enthusiasts are here, so he might have come too."

"*Ah! Bonjour, cher Georges!*" cried a young guards officer, seizing him by the hand. "What brought you here? Anyway, I'm pleased to see that you changed your mind and finally decided to make an appearance in society. I mean, up to now you couldn't even bear the idea. It's very nice here, isn't it? *Magnifique, n'est ce pas?* Let's go, I'll introduce you to Rautov, Svetov, Balov. Very nice fellows! They like you without even having met you, and they always complain that you are in hiding. With all you have going for you, you should really come out of your shell. Let's go! Oh, and by the way, shall I see you on Friday at the Austrian ambassador's?"

"At the Austrian ambassador's? Are you out of your mind? It will be the same thing…"

"Pretty much, *mon cher*, the same crowd… except the imperial family…"

"Don't talk nonsense! I'd just like to know whether you will be coming to my place for dinner. I sent you an invitation."

"What are you up to? Are you planning a surprise? You haven't been left an inheritance, have you? But just a moment! You're looking rather pale, under the weather… No, I bet that's it: you've come into an inheritance and are trying not to look smug… If that's the case, you shouldn't have come – what will people say?" he whispered to him in his ear, and hurried off to meet a lady entering with a young woman. Aduyev was moving around and constantly bumping into people he knew, who inevitably asked him the same questions. "Oh, so you're here?…" "What made you come?" "Isn't this a surprise?" "Back in society?"

He finally decided he had had enough of this, left the reception and went into some neighbouring rooms. "All this is too grand for a public ball," he thought. "Whichever way you turn there's marble and bronze. And what furniture! It's just as if only yesterday some grandee was living here – that's obvious from the decor and the luxurious furnishings of the rooms. Why, there's even a picture gallery!"

Peering through his lorgnette at the paintings he gasped: there were works of Italian painters of all schools, most of them famous – all original. "What does this mean?" he exclaimed. The collection included portraits of the emperor and the empress – excellent works! Next to them was a portrait of some general in a foreign uniform. He looked around to see if there was anyone he knew, in order to ask them who it was. But there was no one, and he started looking at a group of statues. His practised eye immediately fell on a superb sculpture. There were busts of the imperial couple on a raised dais. Opposite them, also on a dais, stood a bust of the same general.

"Who is that?" he asked an English acquaintance who happened to be passing.

"The King of Naples," his acquaintance replied, and disappeared into the crowd.

"Why was the Commercial Club so interested in a Neapolitan king? One would have thought an English king would have been more likely… Well, after all, England is a trading nation. Strange! Oh yes, now I've got it. Of course, the club is renting the premises, including the furnishings. Now it makes sense!"

Meanwhile, the distant sound of music and the crowds bustling around him led him to the hall. At the door he was met by the same old man, who enquired politely why he wasn't dancing.

"Thank you for asking. I never dance," he replied laconically.

"Why is he hanging around me?" Yegor Petrovich muttered as he moved away. "Looks as if he has taken a liking to me. But no, there he is dancing attendance on some others. I guess he's just a friendly type. Quite a few old men like to buttonhole people… You see people like that quite often at public events. I should find out who he is."

But he could see no one he knew, and there was a lull in the dancing. Aduyev was leaning with his back against a marble column, and happened to be looking idly around him thinking of nothing in particular. Suddenly he felt a stabbing pain in his heart: the worm of despair was wriggling in his breast amid the joyfulness of the splendid ball, which only served to exacerbate his loneliness: he was in no mood for merrymaking or mindless enjoyment. Everyone else was carried away by the excitement of the ball. He alone was not enthralled – in the same way that one member of the audience can see through the tricks of a magician and cannot share the amazement of the crowd. "A ball! A ball!" Aduyev thought. "That can keep people's minds busy for a whole week! If it was something new, something they had never seen, something unheard of, then I would understand: the prospect of a ball would tickle their curiosity – it would be only human. But to spend a whole week anticipating the pleasure awaiting them and counting the minutes before an event which they have experienced a thousand times and which will be constantly repeated is just pitiful!" Aduyev could not understand the excitement of the young people, and he was right, just as they would not understand his unhappiness if they knew about it, and would scoff at his distress. And they too would be right.

But let's take a look at what had happened to Aduyev. His eyes, which had been wandering distractedly, suddenly stopped moving, and were focused avidly on one particular sight. He was dumbfounded. He was stunned and could hardly breathe. What sight could have captured his whole attention and so upset him? And at a ball, of all places! Yelena was the only one who could have such an effect on him. Am I telling you that on this occasion it was not she who was having such an effect on him? It was precisely her, pale, sad and sitting next to an Etruscan vase, and barely responding to the kind attentions of three dandies.

"Yelena!… And so miserable… My God! Her, so unhappy!" Such were the thoughts flashing like lightning through Yegor Petrovich's head. From his heart there issued a howl of reawakened love – a voice of sympathy cried out more loudly than ever before, because he had never seen her in such a wretched state.

He saw three of her admirers drifting away from her. They no longer recognized the usual friendly and unfailingly pleasant Yelena, and attached themselves to Countess Z— like tails to a comet. She sat there alone, her eyes no longer sparkling with the old triumphant self-confidence – they were on the brink of shedding tears. She regarded the crowd and the hustle and bustle of that meaningless activity with disdain. That was not what she needed now: what she did need was the embrace and the consoling words of friendship, the warmth of her mother's heart – her mother, to whom she could confide all her anguish. But where was her mother? She was sitting among those resplendent old ladies and like them enjoying the ball, as unaware of her suffering as all the others – like them, entranced by the atmosphere of the ball, a trance from which it would take her a good three days after the ball to wake up. Who was there to give her a sympathetic look? The fact was that there was only one human being alive who understood her, and whose heart beat only for her – and what a heart! But now that one heart had been wounded by her of all people. It was unbearable! Her eyes were idly focused on the crowd as she watched what was going on around her. Finally she looked up, transferring her attention to the columns, which she appeared to be counting. After ending her count, there seemed to be nothing left to look at. But what could be the matter? It was precisely what had been happening to Yegor Petrovich. Why did those eyes, plunged deep in thought, so suddenly sparkle like lightning once again? Why did tears suddenly appear in her eyes and glisten like diamonds on her eyelashes? She could hardly restrain herself from crying out, and struggled to avoid making a spectacle of herself. What did this mean? What it meant was that she had seen Aduyev. The realization that he had not fallen out of love with her, that he had cast aside his usual inhibitions and overcome his aversion to the noisy turbulence of the crowd and the bedlam and had come here in order to see her and to make up with her in the hope of retrieving what he thought he had lost was a thought which brightened up her face with a joy she had never before experienced, triumphant as she was in her victory. That was the reason for her tears – that was why she forgot society, the crowd and propriety itself and focused her passionate, imploring eyes on that young man.

One look at her and he understood everything. What further evidence did he need to know that he was loved? Her pallor, her sorrow, and what seemed to him a courageous action – her appearance at the club – were only too eloquent, and her gaze only completed her victory, a victory not over the mawkish heart of a ballroom peacock, but over a heart still smarting from her wounds. Triumph, my beauty!

"Did she come here just to see me?" Yegor Petrovich was delighted at the thought. "But how did she know? Probably she asked around. So she was unhappy? Oh yes, she loves me – no doubt about it!" He approached her beaming with happiness.

"I'm sorry, *Georges*!" she murmured. "It's all my fault! Forgive me, and forget what I have said and done... pay no attention to what I was saying... it was only because I was annoyed and my pride was hurt. I love you as I have never loved before, but I didn't know it. It's the first time I have ever lost something I loved and suffered for it. Forgive me! It pains me to have wounded someone... especially someone I love... someone without whose forgiveness I haven't known a moment free from guilt. Oh, if only you can forgive me, how much I will learn to love you, to cherish your happiness – happiness I so thoughtlessly tossed aside! You have taught me a lesson – and self-respect..."

Yelena turned away from him in order to hide the tears which were welling in her eyes and about to gush forth, as they do whenever a woman is in such a state. She spoke quickly, in a broken voice. Not understanding her own or anyone else's heart, she wavered between fear and hope, and dared not guess his answer. She was only a girl – a real woman might have acted differently in her situation, although the result would have been the same. You need to have the right skills, Yelena Karpovna. You are still a young woman, my lady! Go and ask the countess – she could advise you.

Aduyev's face paled; his grief had been unbearable, but this sudden onrush of happiness was overpowering.

"Not another word! Have pity on me, Yelena! I can't bear it! I'm sick – my strength is failing me!"

After saying this, he sat down quietly on the chair next to her. At this moment Yelena could only guess the answer, and wanted to look straight at him, but he was gazing at the ceiling, which was covered with frescos (the sky of the ballroom was a beautiful one, especially for those who were present – they could not have wished for a better one), a whole world of mythological gods with Cupid among them, who appeared to be smiling as he reached out to crown her with a garland of myrtle, as a sign of her triumph.

Lucky Aduyev! He must be in seventh heaven right now! His transport of delight is making it hard for him to breathe, speak or even think. He is sitting motionless and pale, unable even to appreciate his blissful state. His thoughts are somehow frozen, blended into a single feeling of boundless joy. "She loves me!" He is struck dumb.

The irritating, addle-pated old man came up to ask him if he was feeling unwell, and whether he needed a bit of air, *fleurs d'orange, des sels...**

"No thanks, I don't need anything!" he said, pulling himself together. "Yelena," he whispered to her. "Right now I have an apology to make. I alone am to blame for everything. I'm more experienced than you and should not have acted the way I did – losing my temper like a boy of seventeen. Now you can treat me twice as coldly, be ten times more capricious and difficult, and I'll bear it all!"

He rose to his feet.

"Where are you going?"

"To the baron, to ask for your hand."

"Right now? Should you? You've already drawn too much attention."

"The least you can do is to get your mother to return home as soon as possible."

It wasn't easy to drag the baron away from his whist and the baroness from her old lady friends. Aduyev put them in a carriage, deposited them at their porch and went in with them.

"Baron, I am asking for the hand of Yelena. All I need to complete my happiness is your consent."

"Pah, this is not a good time! Why didn't you think of it before? Can't it wait until tomorrow morning? You've interrupted our game! I was really stuck into it – and I was winning! I had the ace and king in my hand, and the admiral had—"

"Please don't delay my happiness for one minute! I can't leave without knowing that Yelena is mine."

"Why not? I love you like a son, and have been looking forward to this, and my wife too... What does Yelena say?"

"*Papa!*" she implored him. "*Faites ce qu'il vous demande, je le veux bien!*"*

"That's what she says! You must have read her mind? So be it!"

The parents gave their daughter their blessing. The young couple now were in the same wing, in the same room, where only a few hours before he had been rejected. There's an old proverb which says that dwelling on the past is bad luck. But Yegor Petrovich was still brooding.

"I've suffered so much!" he said, taking her by the hand, "and you tormented me for so long, and in this very place where you so light-heartedly insulted me. Oh, it's so easy for you to gloss it over!"

He moved closer; she looked at him, and, with a smile on her face, lowered her eyes in embarrassment and grew red in the face. Both of their hearts were beating fast – they were finding it hard to breathe. Finally he leant forward a little, intending just to touch her flushed cheeks with his lips, but she averted her head, and her luxuriant, fragrant locks brushed the young man's face, and then turned her head again playfully, so that his lips were still striving for their reward. She stopped moving her head, and looked at him somewhat indecisively, almost at a loss, but with a smile. Their eyes were shining with happiness. They stood there motionless for a short while. An invisible electric charge seemed to thread through their gazes, bringing them closer. Their eyes closed, and their lips met... He stood rooted to the spot, felt his heart miss a beat, and with a shudder knelt and covered her hands with kisses.

"Now, now, that's quite enough for the first time!" said the baron, standing in the doorway. "It's time for supper."

The young couple sprang apart like two pigeons startled by a gunshot.

"No... er... we... you see, sir..." he blurted out, standing there sheepishly like a schoolboy and running his fingers through his hair, while Yelena began to busy herself with her music at the piano.

"Supper time..." he said plaintively. "Do you really want to eat?"

"Well, of course. And I would advise you to do the same. You've interrupted the game of whist when the admiral... Ah, I'll never forget that. And now you are trying to make me miss supper too? Not on your life!"

Having once more discerned the happiness in Yelena's eyes, Aduyev again covered her hands with kisses and rushed off home. I won't even attempt to describe in what state he was... He wasn't actually engaged, but we have to assume that he was in a good mood. Still wearing his hat, he made straight for his study, where he found his valet Yelisei. But the old man was still put out by the unkind comment made earlier by his master. Yegor Petrovich sensed this. "Yelisei," he said, "I'm afraid I offended you today. I'm sorry! Please don't be angry! I give you my word that it will never happen again." Yelisei first stared open-eyed at his master, and then dropped to his knees and kissed his hand.

"Dear Yegor Petrovich," he began, "I'm only here to serve you. I served your father for thirty years, and was by his side during the Turkish campaign. I've known many gentlemen in my time, but I've never seen anything so weird as a master apologizing to his servant!"

"But surely it isn't shameful to admit that one is at fault and try to make amends? Furthermore, you are no longer my servant: I am granting you your freedom and awarding you a pension."

"My freedom! Are you really so angry with me? I'm alone in the world. Where can I go to lay my wretched head? I've always lived under your roof, and expect to die here, if you don't grudge an old man a crust of bread. Your offer is very kind, but who cares? I looked after you when you were a child, and served alongside your late father in the Turkish campaign..."

"Now live your own life the way you want! Surely it's time for you to rest from your labours... You're no longer in my service. Here, please take this at least!" he said, handing him a wallet containing money. Yelisei looked at it on one side and then turned it over to inspect the other side, then shook his head and placed it on the table.

"Dear Yegor Petrovich, sir! Why would I want this? With God's mercy and your kindness, I really have no need of it; I'm fed, clothed and shod while there are so many others out there dirt-poor and without a crust of bread! Don't send me away! As long as I have the strength and my legs hold out, I'll never stop serving you and making myself useful. How can some young fellow know how to look after you the way you expect? I was the one who cared for you, and served your father and was at his side in the Turkish campaign..."

"You are an honourable man, Yelisei! God will reward you. Now listen to me, I have some news for you, old—"

"But, sir! Why do you say 'old'?" he asked hurriedly.

"Old boy!..."

"Phew! My heart sunk for a moment! I thought that, God forbid, you were going to say 'old devil'!"

"Here's the good news – it will make you happy: I'm going to marry Yelena Karlovna."

"Oh my! That's good news indeed! I thank God that I've lived to enjoy such happiness!"

The old man crossed himself, with tears in his eyes, and once again sank to his knees before Aduyev and kissed his hand.

"My congratulations, sir! If only the baron and my dear mistress, your mother, were alive now, God rest their souls!" The old man once again crossed himself reverently and looked at the icon. "I wish you happiness – God should be thanked for his benevolence! God did not see fit to let them live to see this – yet a miserable sinner like me, he deemed worthy! Congratulations, sir! I'm going to tell everyone!" The old man wiped a tear from his eye with his palm and, stumbling, rushed out of the room.

Aduyev struggled to fall asleep that night, and the next morning, earlier than usual, started to dress in order to hurry where his heart beckoned and where he was expected. When he was dressed and ready, he picked up his hat and went out into the hall. In front of the porch a grey trotter was waiting restlessly, snorting and kicking up the snow with its hoof as if he shared his master's impatience. A servant threw a fur coat over Yegor Petrovich and opened the door when suddenly, like a mushroom emerging from the ground, his bald manager appeared carrying a great pile of papers. He bowed low and stood on the porch.

"What is it, Yakov?"

"There are some matters for you to attend to, sir."

"What matters?"

"Yesterday, you told us that when anyone had anything to report, they should come and see you."

"Did I? I really don't remember," he said, moving towards the door.

"But sir... You said: 'Be sure to show me every document, I want to see everything.'"

"Well, I may have done... Can't it wait?"

"No sir! I have written a response to the peasants' petition – and to the two lads who are being drafted... "

"Oh yes, I remember now!" said Yegor Petrovich. "The responses were no good. Tell them that arrears no longer have to be paid."

"But sir, it's eighteen thousand roubles!" The manager was alarmed.

"It doesn't matter," Yegor Petrovich replied calmly. Yelisei and Yakov shook their heads. "Furthermore I want you to take ten thousand of mine and donate it to the poorest. And give some money to the two conscripts. Give one of them a thousand roubles for his wedding and for sustenance, and the same amount to the other one to support his family. As for the gardener, I'll buy the seeds myself, and write to tell the architect to see that the work on the house is finished by June – I'll be sending the furniture and the rest myself."

After delivering these words, Aduyev moved quickly towards the door.

"Excuse me, sir! There's something else! They've written from the Orlov estate to say that they've used up all their corn – there's been a great demand. Would you like them to start using their reserves? The estate manager writes... Let me read it to you... "

Yakov put on his metal spectacles and started rummaging through the stack of papers until he found a greasy letter, and, when he had finished coughing, began: "I would like to wish our kind master, our dear Yegor Petrovich, long life, and inform him that Fomka and Garaska Lapchuk, Fadey Gorshenkov, Mishka Trofimov and his father together with Trofim Yevdokimov on ten carts... "

"Stop making a fool of yourself, Yakov Tikhonych!" said Yelisei. "Look where Yegor Petrovich is!" He pointed to the street outside the window: Aduyev was already well on his way.

Seeing Yakov's preparations before starting to read – a complicated operation which threatened to last a good half hour, Yegor Petrovich had slipped away in his usual manner. The same trotter he had used the day before was moving at top speed and flying like an arrow along the Nevsky Prospekt. "Get a move on!" Aduyev shouted repeatedly.

"Reckless fool! You're going to crash!" passers-by told him as he whizzed by.

"So what do you say, Yelisei Petrovich? It's not a joke! He's cancelled their debt of eighteen thousand and given them an additional ten thousand of his own money – twenty eight thousand in total! Not to mention the money he's giving to save those two lads from being drafted! He's splashed out two thousand – and what on earth for? Just imagine, over two thousand gone in a moment! He must have been taking too much snuff!"

"Not like his late father, I'll tell you that!"

"He's only human, you know..."

"What are you saying, Yakov Tikhonych?"

"I swear it's true."

The old fellows offered each other tobacco and parted. Aduyev returned home after all the guests invited the day before had already arrived. Among them was Brodsky, who had got his ticket for the Commercial Club ball.

"A fine way to behave! You promised to be at the club, but where were you? Tell me! And why didn't you tell me there was a ball? I have to say, I didn't expect such extravagance."

"Well, really!" said the other. "Wasn't I the one who spent the whole evening waiting for you at the entrance to the hall? Why didn't you even take the trouble to show up? We should have met here. I can't understand how we could have missed each other. And why would you think there was anything exceptional about the decor? After all your own premises are just as grand…"

"For goodness' sake! Servants in velvet and gold. Everything glittering, and marble and bronze everywhere! Not to mention the lighting and the furnishings! An entire picture gallery! What a distinguished gathering, such good taste! And everyone so elegantly dressed! It took my breath away! Why, it could have been an ambassador's reception, it was so—"

"Servants in velvet… marble… bronze … such good taste… everyone so elegantly dressed…" Bronsky couldn't get over it. "Come on! What are you talking about? What society? Did you see courtiers there, or the diplomatic corps?"

"All of them, my friend! And Countess Z— and R—! All the smart set. Why don't you ask Druzhevsky? He was there too. Isn't that so, Druzhevsky? Weren't all the ambassadors and the cream of St Petersburg society at the ball yesterday evening?"

"Yes, they were all there."

"And what ball was it, if I may ask?" said Bronsky.

"The one where we were with Aduyev, at the Neapolitan ambassador's."

"Congratulations!" they all shouted, laughing. "You went from one extreme to the other! As usual, no one invited you, and you showed up anyway!"

The young people started laughing and joking – Aduyev called for the driver and asked him where he had taken him yesterday.

"Where you told me to: to the ball on the English Embankment. There's always a lot of carriages waiting and lights in all the windows whenever you pass by. I guessed that must be the place."

Aduyev burst out laughing along with the others at this naive explanation, especially when he realized that the "addle-pated old man" who was hovering around him was none other than his host, the Neapolitan envoy.

Raising the first glass of champagne (you will have noticed that I didn't use the word "cup": that would have been an anachronism: in a gathering of young unmarried men champagne is not drunk from cups)...*

Raising the first glass of champagne, Yegor Petrovich proposed a toast to the health of Baroness Yelena Karlovna Neyleyna, his fiancée. The young men were roused to action: they jumped onto the chairs and drank to the health of the lucky young woman. There was a lot of tomfoolery that day. To the envoy Yegor Petrovich offered his apologies, and since the ambassador knew the baron, he was happy to make his acquaintance, and in gratitude for his attendance at the ball, he promised to come to his wedding – to which I hereby invite my readers.

AN EVIL MALADY

(1838)

In December 1830, when cholera was still to be
found in Moscow, but significantly diminished, of
two hundred and fifty chickens, fifty were to perish
within an extremely short period of time.

Scientific paper on the effect of cholera in
Moscow, Dr Christian Loder, Moscow, p. 81.

H AVE YOU READ, dear sirs, or at least heard about the strange illness that was to afflict children in Germany and France, an illness that had no name and that was hitherto unknown in medical records – namely, their inexplicable urge to go and visit St Michael's Mount (in Normandy, I believe)?

All attempts on the part of the desperate parents to stop them were in vain: the slightest resistance to the children's pathological wish and their lives, very sadly, slowly began to fade away. Isn't that astonishing? Not being acquainted with medical literature, and not having followed its discoveries and successes, I am unable to tell you whether this fact has been explained, or at the very least its probability confirmed. But I, for my part, would like to tell the world about a similar and equally strange and incomprehensible epidemic of whose devastating effects I myself was to be a witness and of which I very nearly became a victim. In presenting my observations in every possible detail I make so bold as to warn my readers that such observations cannot be subjected to any doubt – even though, regrettably, they would not be scientifically approved by medical experts.

Before beginning to describe this illness with all its symptoms I consider it my duty to inform the reader of those particular people who had the misfortune to be afflicted by it.

Several years ago I became acquainted with the lovely, kind-hearted and educated Zurov family and began spending practically every winter evening with them. Time passed imperceptibly within this family, within the circle of their acquaintances and with the range of pleasurable entertainments which they chose and permitted to take place in their house. There were, it is true, no playing cards, and had an idle old man, or indeed a spoilt young man tormented by intellectual or spiritual emptiness, sought for monetary gain or some kind of distraction from gambling, they would have been disappointed: their hopes and aspirations would never have coincided with the noble and high-minded way of life of the Zurovs and their guests. But, on the other hand, the winter evenings would be taken up with dancing, music and, above all, with reading and discussions about literature and art.

I look back with considerable pleasure on this densely packed crowd of friends as they sat around a large table; in front of it there was a Turkish divan, on which our good-natured hostess, Mariya Alexandrovna, would be ensconced dispensing tea, while Alexei Petrovich himself, usually with a cigar and a cup of cold tea in his hands, would be ambling around the room, stopping every so often to join in a conversation and then resuming his stroll. I can also remember the eighty-year-old grandmother, sitting chairbound some distance apart from everyone in a secluded corner, lovingly observing all her offspring, her already semi-blind eyes clouded by salt tears of contented happiness. I can remember the way she would keep on calling over to her youngest grandson Volodya for him to come up to her so that she could stroke his hair – something that was not always to the frisky young lad's liking, and he would often pretend that he hadn't heard her. Above all, grandmother was a quite extraordinary person in many ways, so I hope I can be allowed to say a little bit more about her. She would sit there, as I have already described, always in the same place, able to move only her left hand. But you would be amazed by what she could do with that one hand! By her ability to use just the single palm of one hand for the benefit of all those present! As a consequence, despite her fading powers and the barely perceptible spark in such a frail and ancient vessel, she formed an honourable link in the chain of being. When her grandchildren picked her up from her bed in the morning and placed her in her armchair, she would open the blind on the window with her left hand with such loving and motherly care that woe betide anyone else who tried to stop her! But that wasn't all! I can't refrain from mentioning her most important attribute, something which the poor mass of mankind find very difficult to master: to use a severe disability such as paralysis to advantage. And Grandmother did just this. The fact was that she served as the family's living barometer: she was able at any time to predict the weather. Thus, if Mariya Alexandrovna, Alexei Petrovich or any of the older grandchildren needed to go outside, they would ask her: "Mother (or Grandma), what's the weather going to be like?" And like some inspired Sybil she would touch one of her paralysed limbs and reply succinctly and to the point: "Snow... fine... thaw... hard frost", depending on the circumstances – and she was never wrong. The family were so lucky to have such a treasure in their midst! There was also, I remember, a distinguished retired professor of political economy, whose study of the different effects of various sorts of snuff was much to the enrichment of mankind. Finally, I can remember sitting next to one of the Zurovs' nieces, the sensitive, thoughtful Fyokla, with whom I loved to converse quietly on various topics, including, for example, how long stockings could last after they have been darned, or what length of linen I would need for a new shirt and so on, to which she would always give clear and satisfying answers. I can remember the witty but never caustic or hurtful comments flying everywhere, awakening the outbursts of friendly laughter – I can remember... But forgive me, ladies and gentlemen, my inability to clarify and set out all my memories in any kind of decent order: they are jostling around so tightly in my head, forcing tears from my eyes which roll down my cheeks and blot my writing paper. Permit me to wipe them away – otherwise you will never hear the end of my story...

So I can now calmly revert to my topic, from which I have been sidetracked by my emotion and fellow feeling. "Fellow feeling?" I hear you ask... "What?... Why?... What do you mean?" Yes, fellow feeling, precisely that, ladies and gentlemen – profound fellow feeling. I was connected to my group of acquaintances not only by spiritual, but also heartfelt emotional links, links that I wanted to make as secure and official as possible. Do you remember that reference to my conversation with Fyokla? That wasn't just a chance reference... hmm! How can I not weep, how can I not be in torment when I think that the entire family, beginning with the grandmother and finishing with the reprobate Volodya, was to perish, perish irrevocably as the victims of a terrible epidemic – which, fortunately, ended with them, even though it could well have also afflicted their acquaintances?

I began by mentioning that I had spent the winter evenings at the Zurovs' house, but I said nothing about the summer evenings, because I spent the summers away from St Petersburg, at the invitation of my old uncle, to live with him in the country and imbibe, at his insistence, his home-made concoctions. The rowanberry liqueur could help, as he maintained, restore my nervous system, while his soured and fermented milk speciality, his favourite midday tipple, could prevent the stomach ailments to which I was prone at the time. I made three whole trips in a row to the countryside for a health cure, as if taking the waters, but on the fourth occasion fate intervened to inflict two terrible catastrophes on the province where my uncle lived: the first was a collapse of the berry harvest, as a consequence of which the liqueur bottles remained empty and idle, and the second was a cattle plague, so devastating that the number of cattle, three hundred and fifty in all, declined to just three, drastically affecting the yield of soured and fermented milk. Seeing the wide world gradually losing its charm and his favourite pastimes biting the dust, my uncle died from grief along with his last, favourite cow, leaving the estate to me. Spending the rest of that summer sorting everything out, I returned to St Petersburg at the beginning of winter. My first visit was, naturally, to the Zurovs. They were overjoyed to see me. Everything was just as it had always been, and the winter evenings resumed their normal pattern: the very same faces in the Zurovs' warm and cosy room, sitting as usual at tea around the very same table – with me once again sitting next to Fyokla, Alexei Petrovich with his cigar and Mariya Alexandrovna, with her customary kindness and wit, engaged as ever and seemingly interminably embroidering on her canvas, something that she had begun before her marriage. Only the children had changed somewhat: the older son had grown up, gone to university and started to keep alert for the rustle of a female skirt, while the younger had stopped hiding his snuffbox in a handkerchief with his German tutor and seating his grandmother between the armchairs, while the grandmother herself had further extended her repertoire, absent-mindedly lowering the blind in the middle of the day or raising it as she was going to sleep. Nonetheless, all the rest was the same as ever.

The winter passed quickly; the evenings became shorter; Grandmother stopped predicting hard frosts – she could be heard more and more frequently uttering the word "thaw". April arrived; the sun's bright rays heralded the last day of winter – which, as it departed, made such a mournful face that the River Neva nearly died from laughing and burst its banks, while the frozen ground smiled through the snow. The frivolous chirping of the swallow and the upward flight of the lark announced the arrival of spring. The air became filled with its customary sounds: things which had died or gone to sleep were resurrected and woke up again; everything started to come alive, to sing, to leap about, to growl, to quack – both in the heavens above and on the earth below,* both in the waters and under the earth. In this way the residents of St Petersburg came to realize that it was spring.

On that first warm day I set off cheerfully from my house to go straight to the Zurovs to congratulate them on the arrival of spring and to spend the whole day with them.

"Good morning, Alexei Petrovich!" I said. "Greetings, Mariya Alexandrovna! Spring has arrived! It's now very warm."

No sooner had I uttered these words – I grow cold all over at the thought of it – than the entire family suddenly became uncharacteristically transformed: Alexei Petrovich yawned and gave his wife a significant look; she responded with a sickly smile; the two younger children started leaping about convulsively, while the older two began clapping their hands; the grandmother's eyes suddenly lit up in an unnatural way, and everything they said and did seemed to contain something close to wild, euphoric abandon.

"How are you?" I asked finally and timidly. "I hope you're well?"

"Thanks be to the Lord," Alexei Petrovich replied, with a big yawn.

"But there seems to be something strange going on. Has something sad happened, perhaps?"

"No, no, not at all! On the contrary, we're so happy at the arrival of spring: the time has come to begin our walks in the country. We love to take in the fresh air, and we'll be spending most of the summer in the country."

"Wonderful!" I said. "I hope you will allow me to share that pleasure with you."

Once again the same reaction.

"Happily," Alexei Petrovich replied, giving me a wild look. I took serious fright at this, not knowing what to do and how to explain it all. I stood there undecided. But a moment later everything resumed its normal course, and my hostess's welcoming attitude reassured me.

"You'll be having dinner with us this evening, I hope?" she asked.

"With pleasure," I replied, "but since it's still a little early, I trust you'll allow me to go and see someone first."

"Off you go!" Alexei Petrovich shouted after me. "Just make sure to come back, and since you've promised to join us on our out-of-town trips, we'll be able to decide when and how we can organize the first one."

"It's still rather early to be thinking about such trips," I thought to myself, but decided not to say anything, seeing how much they had taken the idea to heart.

Once on my own, I began to cast about in my mind the reasons for the entire family's incomprehensible behaviour.

"Could it be that they've taken against me for some reason?" I wondered. But the invitation to dinner and the friendly words as I was leaving the house ran counter to the strange way they had greeted me. What could this all mean? As I mulled this all over, I suddenly had the idea of going to see an old acquaintance to find out what was going on... Oh, yes! I forgot to say that included among the Zurovs' guests were two people whom I should introduce to the reader immediately, as they are to play a significant role in this whole business.

One of them was Ivan Stepanovich Verenitsyn, a retired state councillor,* a great friend of the Zurovs since childhood. He generally seemed preoccupied with something or other. He cut a rather gloomy figure, and only rarely took part in the general conversation, always sitting some distance away from the others or pacing about the room in silence. Many people took umbrage at his unsociable attitude and started to spread unpleasant rumours about him: it was said that he found life repugnant and that he had once tried to drown himself, but some peasants had pulled him out of the water, for which they had been awarded the St Anna Medal.* One old woman maintained that he consorted with the Devil, and everyone generally said he suffered from pride and took him to task for his scornful attitude towards the world, while there were some who divulged it as a great secret – there are such nasty people in the world! – that he was in love with a woman of dubious reputation. In short, if you believed everything that people said about him, you had no choice but to dislike him. If, on the other hand, you didn't believe it, then you hated the others for slandering him in that way. I didn't belong to either camp, and I was later to see that his behaviour was a consequence of a particular way of looking at the world and certain observations about it which, if he wanted to, he could have made public himself. But we had no business to meddle in someone else's business: we didn't need to know anything other than the fact that he was at the Zurovs every day and enjoyed their special affection.

The other figure was my university friend, Nikon Ustinovich Tyazhelenko, a Little Russian landowner,* also an old acquaintance of the Zurovs – it was through him that I had got to know the family. This Tyazhelenko had, ever since childhood, gained a reputation for an unparalleled and deliberately chosen lifestyle of idleness and of heroic indifference to the vanities of this world. He spent the greater part of his life lying in his bed. If he sometimes got up, it was simply to take his seat at the dinner table. Doing the same for breakfast and supper was, in his opinion, not worth the effort.* As I have already said, he rarely left home, and with his sedentary, not to say prone, way of life, he acquired all the attributes of a lazy man: he proudly sported a magnificent belly of enormous size; flabby folds enveloped his entire body, like a rhinoceros, forming a kind of natural clothing. He lived right next to the Tauride Garden,* but for him to go for a walk there was an extraordinary feat. His doctors' warnings that he would inevitably be afflicted by a whole legion of illnesses and risk many different kinds of death unless he did something about his condition were totally ignored: he rejected their exhortations in the simplest and clearest ways. If, for example, they took him to task for hardly ever walking anywhere, which made him vulnerable to an apoplectic stroke, he replied that there was a dark passage connecting his entrance hall with his bedroom along which he walked no less than five times a day – which, in his opinion, was absolutely, totally sufficient to avert a stroke. And he would add in conclusion the following reasoned argument: even if he were to suffer a stroke, he would as a consequence be able, perfectly legitimately, to stay at home the whole time without leaving the house. This served as the most eloquent of defences against any attacks on him, and therefore he had nothing to fear so far as his health was concerned. As for the fresh air he was prescribed to take, he maintained that, on waking up in the morning, he would press his face against the open window pane and spend the whole day sucking in the fresh air. His doctors and friends shrugged their shoulders and left him in peace. That was my friend Nikon Ustinovich. He loved the Zurovs and visited them once a month, but when that seemed more than he could manage, he deliberately introduced me to them.

"Go and see them as often as you can, old boy," he said to me. "They are wonderful people, and I love them to bits. But they expect me to go and see them every week – would you believe it?! So, please, go on my behalf and tell them what I've been doing, and bring me their latest news."

It was to him, to Tyazhelenko, that I went after the Zurovs had behaved so strangely, in the hope that he, as an old acquaintance of theirs who knew everything about them, would be able to explain it to me. At the precise moment that I dropped in to see him, he was contemplating turning over onto his left side.

"Hello, Nikon Ustinovich," I said. Lying there, he nodded. "Are you well?" He nodded again, in affirmation: Nikon Ustinovich was never one to waste words. "The Zurovs send their regards, and complain that you clearly don't love them any more."

He shook his head as a sign of denial.

"Well, say something then, old friend, even if it's only a couple of words."

"Wait a bit... I need a moment to myself, if you would," he finally said very slowly. "They'll be bringing my breakfast shortly, so I'll be sitting up, perhaps."

Five minutes later his servant with some difficulty delivered to Nikon Ustinovich's table what he had modestly referred to as "my breakfast" and that could easily have been enough for four people. The piece of roast beef was so large that it hardly fitted on the plate; a number of eggs threaded the sides of the tray; a cup, or rather a bowl, of hot chocolate was steaming away to one side like the funnel of a boat; lastly, above it all towered a bottle of porter.

"Right then... I'm now..." Tyazhelenko started to say, and tried to sit up, but neither the one nor the other met with success, and he slumped back onto his pillow.

"Surely that's not all for you, is it?"

"No, I'll give some to the dog," he replied, indicating a minute little lapdog, which was lying, no doubt to please, and, in imitation of his master, not moving from the spot.

"Well, let God be the judge of that! But seriously," I continued, "why don't you come with me to have dinner at the Zurovs?"

"What's that? Are you in your right mind?" he said, with a wave of his hand. "Much better to stay here: I've got some glorious ham... there's sturgeon, Siberian dumplings, sausages, pudding, turkey and a wonderful omelette – ordered it to be made in a particular way myself, dear boy."

"No, thank you. I promised them I would go – in any case, they're planning to have an interesting conversation about some out-of-town expeditions over dinner."

Tyazhelenko's face suddenly became alive. Making a tremendous effort, he half sat up in bed.

"So... you too... you too!" we both exclaimed together.

"What do you mean by that remark?" I asked.

"What do *you* mean by it?"

"It comes," I replied, "from my astonishment at seeing the strange, compulsive behaviour of the Zurovs just a moment ago – and now here you are almost leaping out of your skin when I began referring to the spring and expeditions into the country. So now you can see my reason for exclaiming like that. And what was your reason?"

"Mine's more important than yours," he replied, as he stuffed a piece of roast beef into his mouth. "I thought you must have gone down with something."

"Me? Gone down with something? Thank you for your concern, but why should you have assumed that?"

"I thought that... you must have been infected."

"The plot thickens! By whom? With what?"

"By whom? The Zurovs, of course."

"What utter nonsense is this? Please explain, if you would be so kind."

"Wait a moment... let me eat." And he quietly began chewing away at the piece of meat, like a cow. Finally the last piece disappeared. Once everything had been eaten and drunk, the servant, who had brought in the breakfast with two hands, took the remainder away with two fingers. When I moved closer, Tyazhelenko began.

"In the three years you have known the Zurovs, have you noticed anything special about them?"

"Nothing so far."

"Will you be joining with them in their country expeditions in the summer?"

"No, I'll be staying here."

"In that case, starting from this morning, you'll be noticing some very strange goings-on indeed."

"But what on earth does it all mean? Am I going to get any sense out of you? And if there has been something strange going on, why haven't you told me about it before?"

"What it means," Tyazhelenko continued, "is that the Zurovs are ill."

"What are you talking about? How, in what way, are they ill?" I cried in horror.

"It's a very strange, infectious illness, my boy. Sit down, listen, and stop rushing me... In any case, I can already foresee I'm going to get terribly tired. It's such a pain to have to talk so much! But there's nothing for it: I simply have to save you. I've said nothing about any of this before, because there's been no need: you've only been here in St Petersburg during the winter, and there hasn't been anything noteworthy about them in particular – they're such a clever lot... time simply flies by as they chat away. But come the summer, something very strange happens! They're transformed... they become quite different people... they don't eat, they don't drink: they've got just one thing on their minds... It's so sad! So sad! But there's nothing anyone can do to help!"

"Couldn't you at least tell me what sort of disease it is, and what it is called?" I asked.

"It doesn't have a name, because it's very probably the first time it's appeared. As for what kind of disease it is, I'll tell you immediately. It's... what can I say?... How best to begin?... Well, you see... it's not easy, when you don't have a name for it... Well, let's just call it for the moment an 'evil malady', and leave it to the medics to determine what their best name for it would be. The fact is that there is no way that the Zurovs are going to be able to stay at home in the summer: that's the terrible, devastating illness we're dealing with."

Tyazhelenko let out an enormous sigh and made a very sour face, as if someone was trying to remove a particularly tasty morsel from between his teeth. I roared with laughter.

"Really, Nikon Ustinovich! But this... illness... is only a figment of your imagination... You yourself are suffering from a far more dangerous illness: you spend your entire life lying in the same spot – such extreme behaviour will more likely than not prove fatal. Or maybe you're joking!"

"Joking?! It's an illness, my dear boy, a terrible illness! Let me put it more clearly: their irrepressible passion for out-of-town walks in the country will destroy them."

"But it's such a lovely passion! I myself have promised them I'll join them."

"Promised them?" he exclaimed. "Oh, Filipp Klimych, that was such an unfortunate thing to do! What have you done? You're finished!" He nearly burst into tears. "Have you spoken to Verenitsyn about this?"

"Not yet."

"Well, thank God for that! There's still time to make everything right, but you need to listen to me."

I looked at him in bewilderment, but he continued: "You see, I myself, in the bad old days, when I was stupid enough to spend most of the day and even the night walking around everywhere on my two legs (that's youth for you!), wasn't even opposed to the idea of going off into the forest carrying a little something... something like, say... a piece of roast turkey under my arm and a bottle of Malaga in my pocket. I'd spend a hot summer's day sitting under a tree, I'd have something to eat and then lie down on the grass for a bit – and then... well, I went home. But these people are killing themselves with their country walks. It's got to the point – can you imagine! – that, if on one particular summer's day they stay at home, then, as they themselves acknowledge (as I overheard during one of their fits), they become oppressed, weighed down, by something that won't leave them alone: some implacable force drives them out of the city, some evil spirit gets into them, and they..." (at this point Tyazhelenko's voice became particularly animated) "and they start swimming, skipping, jumping up and down and running about everywhere. And when they've done so much swimming, skipping, jumping up and down and running everywhere (how on earth they don't drop dead on the spot, I have no idea!), they start climbing steep hills and clambering down into deep ravines," with Tyazhelenko illustrating each of these actions with an eloquent gesture. "They wade through streams, get stuck in bogs, force their way through prickly bushes, scrabble up high trees. The number of times they've nearly drowned, vanished into abysses, become irrevocably stuck in mud, frozen to death in cold and even – most horribly of all – nearly died from hunger and thirst!"

All this eloquence poured out of Tyazhelenko together with his sweat. Oh, what a wonderful sight he was at that moment! His broad brow was furrowed with noble indignation, his forehead and cheeks were covered in large drops of sweat, which could well have been taken for tears, so inspired and animated was the expression on his face. The golden, classical age of ancient times was reappearing in front of my eyes. Casting around in my mind for fitting parallels of famous men, I hit on the figure of the Roman emperor Vitellius.*

"Bravo! Bravissimo! Wonderful!" I cried.

"Yes, Filipp Klimych," he continued, "a disaster, a real disaster has befallen them! It's good that they still sweat from their exertions: for the moment that's... saving them... but soon this life-giving moisture will dry up from sheer exhaustion, and then what's going to become of them? And the infection has become deep-rooted: it's slowly seeping through their veins and consuming their essential life force. That kind Alexei Petrovich! That generous Mariya Alexandrovna! That revered old grandmother! And those children – those poor young people! Their youth, their flourishing health, their dazzling hopes for the future – all of it will drain away, disappear, in exhaustion, in these extremely demanding activities they themselves have chosen to embark on!"

He covered his face in his hands, but I burst out laughing.

"And all you can do is laugh, you cruel man?"

"But how on earth can I not laugh, dear boy, when you, the most independent and unconcerned man I know – someone who couldn't care less if the whole world were to crash down on his head, who wouldn't open his mouth to ask what the noise was – have spent an entire hour agonizing and sweating away, on the verge of weeping, simply because some people have become devoted to a pleasurable activity that you find abhorrent: walking!"

"You still can't seem to understand that I'm not joking. Surely you yourself saw the ominous signs, didn't you?" he said, with some irritation.

"I'm not sure… I thought… Anyway, what signs do you mean?" I asked.

"Well, what about the constant yawning, the absent-mindedness, the melancholy yearning, the sleeplessness and lack of appetite, the pallor of their faces, covered all over at the same time by those weird blotches, and the strange wild look in their eyes?"

"Well, yes, that was precisely what I came to ask you about."

"So then you need to understand and know that the moment they start remembering the forests, the fields, the swamps and the secluded places, all these signs appear, and they're overcome by this yearning and shaking for as long as this calamitous desire cannot be satisfied. Then they race out of the house without a second glance, just able to grab hold of anything they need, as if spurred and driven on by all the demons in hell."

"But where do they go?"

"Everywhere: within twenty miles or so from St Petersburg there's not a single bush they haven't scoured. I'm not talking about the well-known spots such as Petergof and Pargolovo* that everyone visits: they now seek out little-visited, out-of-the-way places so that they can, you understand, converse with nature, breathe in the fresh air, escape the dust and... goodness knows what else! Just listen to Mariya Alexandrovna: she'll go on at you about all those markets and restaurants, and how stifling they are! Hmm! How unfair! What rank ingratitude! To say that markets and restaurants are stifling, when they're havens of health and peaceful happiness! To feel the urge to escape from the centre, the focal point, of the two richest kingdoms of nature – animals and plants! To feel stifled by the air of precisely those places that have erected altars and mansions devoted to the most delightful of human needs: food! Tell me, if you would, what area of the world can be more magnificent than Haymarket Square,* and what can compare with the natural products, the artistic products, that you can find there? And finally, to feel the need to run away from those delights that are the only things that do not run away from us... the everlastingly young, the ever fresh, strewn daily with new flowers that never fade! Everything else is a mirage, unstable, inconstant – other delights and joys slip away from us the moment we achieve them, whereas here, if something should even think of escaping us, it will fly forward like a well-aimed bullet, in response to a capricious desire, and conquer the audacious heart. Why, for goodness' sake, should all these delights and comforts, these extensive facilities exist, if not for the gratification of one's enjoyment and..."

Noting that Tyazhelenko had started sounding off about the subtleties of gastronomy, a science that he was expounding, both theoretically and practically, with such success, and of which he had furnished me two examples in the course of a single morning, I stopped him in his tracks.

"You have forgotten about the Zurovs," I said.

"What else is there to say about them? They're a doomed family! Just imagine," he continued, "in the course of a single walk Alexei Petrovich will typically cover a distance that is nearly as far as the sum total of all the walks I have ever taken in my entire life. For example, he'll set off from Gorokhovaya Street for the Nevsky Monastery, from there to Kamenny Island, where he'll walk and walk, then he'll cross over to Krestovsky Island, from Krestovsky via Koltovskaya Street on to Petrovsky Island, from Petrovsky on to Vasilevsky Island and so back to Gorokhovaya* – how about that then, eh? And all on foot, at a brisk pace – isn't that just such a horrible idea? And there's more! Sometimes, at dead of night, when everything's lying down resting, rich and poor, animals and… birds…"

"I don't think birds lie down," I remarked.

"All right… well, it doesn't matter. But how dreadful for them! Why should nature deprive them of such an innocent pleasure! Where was I?"

"Birds, you said."

"But weren't you saying that birds don't lie down? Hold on: who else lies down?"

"But could you not, my dear Tyazhelenko, stop going off at tangents like this the whole time? You know, keep to the point a bit more? You'll wear yourself out."

"You're right, you're right. Thank you for reminding me. I think I'll lie down, if that's all right with you – it'll be easier for me." He lay down on his pillows and continued:

"Anyway, sometimes Alexei Petrovich will leap up from bed in the middle of the night, go out onto the balcony and then wake his wife, saying: 'It's such a wonderful night, Mariya Alexandrovna! We should go somewhere!' And suddenly all thought of sleep has disappeared! The entire household leaps out of bed, quickly gets dressed and races off, accompanied by two of their most faithful servants – similarly infected, alas! Or on one occasion, of which I myself was the witness, they're in the middle of having dinner, the most joyous moment of one's existence, between the sauce and the meat course, when one's first pangs of hunger have been satisfied but one's anticipation of further delights has not yet been blunted, and Alexei Petrovich suddenly exclaims: 'Why don't we take the pie and the meat course with us and go out of town?' No sooner said than done. The meat course and the pie fly off to the woods and fields, leaving me to return home alone, with tears in my eyes. In short, never has a follower of the philogynous prophet set off for Mecca with such eager longing, never has an old woman from Moscow or Kostroma so longed to breathe in the holy atmosphere of the Kievan caves."*

"If they're so attracted to nature, why don't they go and live in a dacha, or in the countryside somewhere?"

"They did do that at one time, but the children grew up. Concerns about their education and other important matters kept them in the city. But they aren't the only ones, unfortunately, to be afflicted by this evil malady: they are such special people that there are many who want to get to know them, and those who remain here for the summer have been struck down by it. There's an old professor who is beginning to be affected by this melancholy yearning, is losing his appetite and unable to sleep; several would-be suitors of his niece, Zinaida, have fallen by the wayside, disliking her newly acquired talent for yawning the whole time; and there is one particular diplomat whose charming wife would find life impossible if she didn't go and take the waters every summer."

"It seems to me you've been struck down by it yourself," I said. "All this trivial nonsense is sending me to sleep."

"Go ahead – if that's what you'd like to do, I won't stop you," Tyazhelenko replied with some irritation. "And I equally don't care if you want to believe in it all or not."

"Don't be angry, my dear fellow! Instead, why don't you tell me how you meant to rescue me, and where the source of this sickness is?"

"What? Surely I've told you already, haven't I? Verenitsyn, dear boy: he's the original source! He was the one who infected the Zurovs!"

"Really? But he's so devoted to them—"

"Yes, yes," Nikon Ustinovich interrupted me, "he's a wonderful man, very fond of his food, and all that – but what can one do? About eight years ago he set off for a trip around Russia – he was in Crimea, Siberia, the Caucasus... some people seem to have this yearning to roam about the world! Finally he withdrew from everything and settled down in the Orenburg area,* where he lived for a bit, but about four years ago he came back here, much changed in character and afflicted with this 'evil malady'. He started going round to the Zurovs every day as before, and began gradually to infect their brains and finally succeeded in poisoning them – and the closer people are to them and the more openly they behave with each other, the more likely and easily they are to become infected."

"So how," I asked, "did you yourself find out about the cause of this strange behaviour?"

"From him himself, of course! But he's always reluctant to reply when asked: he turns away from you angrily and mutters through his teeth, 'It's an illness, that's all!' However, the Zurovs' housekeeper, Anna Petrovna, a good friend of mine, told me in strict confidence that apparently, while living in Orenburg, he would often take trips out into the steppes, where he'd fallen in love with some Kalmyk* or Tatar woman, or whatever. You see what type of man he is? You can't get any sense out of him. Try and ask him: 'What did you have for dinner today, Ivan Stepanych?' – he won't say a word: such a tight-lipped individual! Anyway, Anna Petrovna maintains he's lived among these Mongol, nomadic people, where he's fathered two children, whom he hid goodness knows where. Anyway, was it surprising that there, in the middle of the steppes, he should have acquired this penchant for nature and the open country? And the fact that he should have found it all so alluring and seductive is hardly to be wondered at: Asiatic witches were always wiser and more profound than European ones. You've read about the Arabian sorcerers, haven't you? Miracle-workers! Pay him a visit one evening sometime: those accursed creatures give him such looks!"

"What accursed creatures?"

"His kittens, of course! There are two of them always on his lap, two on the table, and two more on his bed. But come daytime, they're nowhere to be seen! Say what you like, there are strange things going on there!"

"And you're not ashamed to believe such rubbish?"

"It's not a question of me believing it: I'm simply recounting Anna Petrovna's suppositions."

"But you still haven't told me why you yourself haven't become infected and whether or not there is some remedy for this disease."

"There's no permanent remedy; each individual has to work out his own. I was warned by the late Colonel Trukhin, who, too, never succumbed to this 'evil malady'. He was nobody's fool, and as soon as Verenitsyn tried to put a spell on him, he felt that something was not quite right and made every effort to avoid being trapped. Luckily, he remembered some poem or other that always cast Verenitsyn into the pit of depression. He would start declaiming this poem, Verenitsyn would pass out and he would be saved. Although Verenitsyn never tried again to destroy the colonel's life, he continued assiduously in his efforts, attempting like some demon-seducer to insinuate himself into people's souls, lulling them to sleep, reducing them to an unconscious state and then hitting them with his magic charm... not sure how exactly – perhaps, get them to eat, or drink, something... Anyway, when he tried to ensnare *me* in his poisonous net, I began thinking up ways how I could thwart him by doing something unusual – as Trukhin had prescribed. I thought and thought, until finally I came up with this idea – guess what?"

"Haven't a clue," I replied.

"Do you remember my voice?"

"Your voice? What are you on about?"

"Surely you remember, don't you? Wait, I'll sing you something." He pursed his lips, puffed up his cheeks and was on the point of filling his little temple with profane sounds when the screech of unoiled wheels suddenly came into my head. My ears ringing with the memory, I flung my arms in the air and yelled at him at the top of my voice:

"Yes, I remember, I remember! Please don't start singing, I beg you! A monstrous voice!"

"All right, all right," he said, "even though my motherland is rightly praised for its melodic voices, and there are even some freaks within the family! Anyway, as soon as he began trying to cast his spell on me, I suddenly started singing at the top of my voice: he put his hands to his ears and disappeared. You'll need to think up something of the sort yourself, but just remember you have to dumbfound him straight away, otherwise that's it, you're finished! Later, the Zurovs themselves conspired to get me involved and persuaded me to go for a walk with them in the Summer Garden,* no doubt with the intention of luring me out of town from there. It wasn't at all easy for them to get me to agree, but eventually we set off. All too aware of their malevolent plan, I began to look around for somewhere to hide, and what do you think? Right there, a couple of yards away, there was a little shop selling sausages! There was no time to think: they'd started chattering away to one another, so I darted into the shop. They had no idea where I'd gone: they looked and looked everywhere, with me watching them from inside through the window, doubled up from laughter! That's all I can tell you about this 'evil malady'. Don't ask me about it again. Look at my face: can't you see in my eyes how much these bitter memories and having to talk about them for so long have upset me? In that case, you'll understand the extent of the sacrifice I have made for the sake of our friendship: stop shattering my peace and calm, and... make yourself scarce. Hey, Bobolenko!" he shouted to his servant. "Water! Pour some over my head, close the blinds and don't disturb me until dinner."

I tried to ask him some more questions, but in vain: he adamantly refused to answer, religiously maintaining a stubborn silence.

"Goodbye, Nikon Ustinych!" He nodded silently, and I left.

"Which one of them is the sick one?" I thought. "Clearly, it's Tyazhelenko. What was all that nonsense he talked about those dear, kind Zurovs? I'll be able to have such a laugh with them about my idle friend!"

I walked around for a little longer, and then went back to the Zurovs. Alexei Petrovich was busy with the older children sorting out some fishing tackle. Mariya Alexandrovna was writing something. I glanced down at the piece of paper and noticed the heading, in large writing: "List of silver plate, tablecloths and crockery required for this summer's trips".

"My goodness!" I thought. "They're getting seriously ready for their walks!"

A little distance away Feklusha was darning her grey stockings with a grey-coloured thread, also preparing for the walks. Mariya Alexandrovna greeted me with a yawn.

"Ivan Stepanych is waiting for you in the billiards room," she said. "It's still a little early, and he would like to give you a game."

Verenitsyn met me with the kind of look a shopkeeper gives when you enter his shop, or a tailor his workshop – that is, with the anticipation of making some money. Suddenly, in the middle of the game, I scrutinized him more intently: he was yawning, and giving me a rather miserable look.

"What is it? What's the matter?" I exclaimed, hurrying over to him.

"It's nothing, carry on playing," he said in a deep bass voice. "Forty-seven to thirty-four."

"No," I replied, "let's finish the game later. I'd like to have a rest now, if you don't mind: I've been for a long walk."

"What a good idea! Let's sit down here, on the sofa, for a bit."

We sat down. I rested my head on the cushion. He bent down to my ear and started to whisper something so quietly that I couldn't make out a word he was saying. I found it rather boring and dozed off.

"Are you asleep?" he asked hurriedly.

"Al... most," I muttered through my sleep.

"Oh, please don't go to sleep! There's so much I need to talk to you about, and I've only just begun..."

"For... give... me... I... simply... can't..."

I don't remember anything else: I fell asleep. All I can remember hearing, through my sleep, was him leaving the room and grumbling, with a sigh: "Failed again! He's fallen asleep, not having listened to me. I'm clearly unable to pass my illness on to anyone else. I'll simply have to drag it around with me for ages and resign myself to having the Zurovs as my only companions!"

I don't know how long I was asleep. One of the servants woke me when everyone else had already sat down at the table.

"'Failed again,' he said," I thought. "Surely Tyazhelenko can't have been right, can he? The poor Zurovs... So it seems that I've manged to escape his devilish snares by lapsing into a well-timed sleep!"

Seated at the dinner table, apart from the Zurovs, was Zinaida with her uncle. At first everyone engaged in lively conversation, but towards the end of the meal Alexei Petrovich started yawning furiously, causing everyone else to follow suit, apart from myself.

"But when are we off into the country?" Alexei Petrovich asked, turning to Verenitsyn.

"The day after tomorrow," he replied.

"Granny," cried Volodya, "what will the weather be like the day after tomorrow?"

"Cloudy," the old woman answered.

"What does it matter, if it is cloudy?" said Mariya Alexandrovna. "We can still go, even if it's raining."

"But please," I exclaimed, "surely you can wait at least until May, can't you? It's still cold, and there's still no grass on the fields. How can you even think of trips into the countryside in April, and in your state of health?..."

"What do you mean? I'm perfectly well, aren't I?" she interrupted me. "I'm quite often well. Don't you remember: on my name day, the day after Boxing Day, three times during Lent, I felt perfectly fine. What else do you want?"

"But won't you be coming with us?" asked Alexei Petrovich. "You gave us your word."

"I am perfectly prepared to partake in this pleasure with you," I replied, "but not before the beginning of June, and certainly not each and every time you plan to go. I don't understand how you

don't get bored going on these out-of-town excursions so often
– what is there to do?"

"How can you say that?" everyone chorused. "What is there
to do!"

And one by one they began to tell me:

"Sit in the sun without a hat, and fish!" yelled Alexei Petrovich
frenziedly.

Fyokla: "Eat butter, plums, pick berries and mushrooms."

Zinaida: "Gaze into the blue sky, breathe in the scent of flowers,
watch the flow of water, wander through the meadows."

Verenitsyn: "Tire yourself out walking around with a pipe in
your mouth, reflect on everything you see, look down deep into
every ravine."

Grandma: "Sit in the grass and chomp raisins."

The older son, student: "Eat stale bread, take sips of water and
read Virgil and Theocritus."*

Volodya: "Climb trees, go bird-nesting and make pipes from
twigs."

Mariya Alexandrovna: "In short, revel in nature in the full sense
of the word. In the countryside the air is fresher, and the scent of
flowers sweeter; out there one's whole body quivers with unknown
delight; the sky is not clouded by dust, rising in clouds from the
stifling city walls and the stinking streets; one's blood circulation
is better balanced, one's thoughts are freer, one's soul lighter and
one's heart purer; out there one can converse with nature in its
temple, in the midst of the fields, become aware of its majesty..."

And she went on and on in this vein! Oh Lord, it was so painful!
I could see, clearly see, that Nikon Ustinych had been right: they
were a doomed family! I sank my head in my chest and said
nothing. And, anyway, what point would there have been in trying
to contradict them? One man can hardly prevail against a whole
crowd, can he?

From that moment onwards I was to become a painful observer
of the progress of this 'evil malady'. At times it occurred to me
that I should try to force them to rid themselves, at least for a

time, of this devilish enchantment, shut and lock the doors just as they were about to set off, or dash off to the most famous doctors, and, after exciting first their curiosity and then their sympathetic understanding, implore them to rescue the unfortunate sufferers. But this would mean breaking with them for ever, because they hadn't entirely lost their reason, and when excursions into the countryside weren't on their agenda they were still the same 'winter Zurovs' – in other words, just as kind and as friendly as in winter.

I shall not begin to weary the reader with a description of all the different manifestations and variations of this 'evil malady': my friend Tyazhelenko's account, which I have conveyed practically as he gave it, contains pretty well all you need to know about this sickness, so that all that remains for me is to append, for the sake of greater clarity and authenticity, a description of one or two trips that are most revealing of my acquaintances' pathological condition.

Each of these excursions was invariably marked by some particular notable incident: now there was a broken axle, with the carriage toppling over to one side and things spilling out of it pell-mell, as if from a horn of plenty (saucepans, eggs, roast meat, men, samovar, cups, walking sticks, galoshes, ladies, pretzels, parasols, knives, forks), now days of rain and exhaustion forced them to seek shelter in a little hut, which also became transformed into a most unusual scene, with its chaotic jumble of calves, small children, little benches, blackened walls, Russians and Chukhna* men, cockroaches, frying pans, plates, Russian and Chukhna women, coats, raincoats, peasants' coats, ladies' hats, bast shoes without straps – everything providing an assortment of such diverting entertainment. Among these larger, more general, events there were a number of smaller and more personal incidents: now one of the children would fall into the water, now Zinaida Mikhailovna would step inadvertently with a slender leg into a muddy ditch... But it's not possible to recount everything that happened in the course of these excursions out into the fields and the forests – and could it have been any different, when these poor, unhappy people themselves deliberately set out in search of such discomforts? I can remember, for example, one particular morning, when the weather was still pretty tolerable, we agreed that that same day, after dinner, we would go to Strelna to look at the palace and the park.* During dinner the sky was covered with a dark, leaden cloud, and there was a rumble of thunder in the distance, then the storm got closer and closer and the rain absolutely poured down. I was at first overjoyed at this, thinking that the walk would have to be abandoned, particularly since the first heavy rainfall diminished, turning into a persistent and prolonged drizzle, but in vain: at about five o'clock a number of rented carriages clattered up to the porch.

"What are these for?"

"What do you mean? To get us to Strelna, of course!"

"But surely you can't be going out in such weather, can you?"

"What about the weather? It's only rain."

"You think that's nothing? But we could get soaked, catch our death."

"So? But we'll be going for a walk, won't we? We've got five umbrellas, seven waterproof raincoats, twelve pairs of galoshes and…"

"And fishing rods!" added Alexei Petrovich.

There was nothing for it. I promised I'd join them and set off. The rain poured down in buckets the entire evening and night, meaning that once we'd got to Strelna we had to give the palace a miss and were compelled to go to an inn, where we had the pleasure of drinking tea of dubious quality, colour and taste and chew pieces of unyielding beefsteak.

From then on I started going to the Zurovs rather less often. I had fallen ill three times as a result of the excursions into the countryside, and in any case I frequently found they were not at home – and, if they were, they were always either in the middle of getting ready for some walk or other, or just recuperating from one – more often than not having fallen ill. Nonetheless, I still hadn't given up hope that they would get better, believing that the advice of friends, the help of doctors and, finally, their declining health would combine to eradicate the root of their disastrous monomania. Alas! I was so cruelly mistaken! The next three manifestations of their illness – or, as they called them, walks – will suffice to show the extent to which these unfortunate people had been afflicted by this "malady".

One evening I called in to see them, and was astonished to be greeted by absolute silence in a household where normally reigned jolly conversation, laughter and the sound of piano playing, all interrupting one another. I asked one of the servants about the reason for the unnatural quiet.

"There's been a disaster, sir," he replied in a whisper.

"Why? What's happened?" I asked in alarm.

"The old lady has gone blind, sir."

"Really? Oh my God! Poor Grandma! Why? What happened?"

"Yesterday, during one of the out-of-town walks, she sat for too long in the heat looking at the sun, and when they got home the dear old lady was unable to see a thing."

Alexei Petrovich met me in the drawing room and confirmed what had been said, adding that he was so sorry for Grandma, particularly since it meant that the trips out of town would now have to stop for a while. I shook my head five times: one shake of the head expressing my sorrow at what had happened to the old lady and the other four my irritation at what Alexei Petrovich had said. "Well," I thought, "at least now they'll have to sit at home for some four days... I'm so pleased: perhaps they'll begin to change their mind." Consoling myself with such thoughts, I returned home and went to bed.

The next morning, at about six o'clock, I was woken by the sound of people talking and footsteps clattering along the pavement, forcing me to jump out of bed. Supposing that there had to be a fire somewhere close by, I looked out of the window onto the street... and what should I see! Alexei Petrovich, hatless, his hair ruffled and with an expression of wild joy in his eyes, as they darted about devouring everything in their sight; the wind was billowing his raincoat out around him, like a sail; in his hands he was holding two fishing rods with all their accompanying equipment; behind him were the children, from the biggest to the smallest, all leaping around, yelling and dashing about the place. I froze on the spot: never before had the "malady" manifested itself in such an extreme form. As I stood there watching them, the entire group stopped in front of my window and started to yawn.

"Where are you thinking of going in such a hurry, and why are you disturbing my neighbour's peace?" I yelled at them animatedly. In view of the fact that they seemed to be behaving in such an odd way, as if they'd been afflicted by some kind of curse, I thought it appropriate, as often happens in such cases, to resort to using a special language when addressing them.

"We're off to Pargolovo, on foot!" they shouted back in a chorus.

"Really? But what about Grandma?"

"Let her be! We couldn't wait any longer – my wife's stayed behind to be with her. Come and join us."

"Have you gone mad or something? It's about eight miles to Pargolovo!"

"So you're not coming?"

"Not for anything in the world!"

"Oh! Oh! Oh!" they yelled, and dashed off. I stood there for a long time watching them go, two large teardrops rolling down my cheeks. "Why has Heaven inflicted such a punishment on them?" I wondered. "Oh Lord, you move in such mysterious ways!"

After about three hours, when the thick mist that had lain over the city since midnight turned into incessant rain and a cold wind came up from the north, my thoughts turned to that group of unfortunate people. I felt so sorry for them that I was simply unable to stand by and coolly leave them to their fate. I hurriedly got dressed and, not knowing a suitable doctor, persuaded a barber to go with me. Together we hired a droshky and set off in pursuit, sensing that they would be in need of help – and I proved to be absolutely right.

There was no sight of them in Pargolovo itself, and from some peasants I learnt that they had gone on some four more miles to some lake, in order to fish, and that they had chosen to take a boggy path rather than the usual road. There was nothing for it but to follow in their tracks. Such tracks soon became clear, in the form of discarded caps and gloves – articles which, in Alexei Petrovich's view, simply got in the way when walking. Finally I found them: Alexei Petrovich was sitting on the bank of the lake with a lacklustre expression in his eyes, his feet dangling in the water up to his knees and holding a fishing rod. He had dozed off, clearly in some semi-delirious state as the blood had rushed entirely from his feet to his head. Next to him lay a perch, its mouth gaping open, and a little further off were the children in various places, slumped in exactly the same position and numb with cold. Their boots were half filled with water, and their clothes soaked from the rain. After half an hour of effort, the barber managed to bring them round, while I dashed off to the nearest village, where I hired three Chukhna peasant carts, in which I placed Alexei Petrovich and the children, covering them with bast matting, and took them back to the city in a desperate condition.

After that little adventure, I didn't call in to see them for a whole two weeks. Eventually, one Sunday morning, I went into the entrance hall. There I found the two infected lackeys, bearing all the malignant signs of the disease, arguing about the best way of breathing in fresh air when going into town – standing on the step behind the carriage, or sitting with the driver on the coach box. "Aha!" I thought. "Things don't look at all good again: they're clearly off on their travels once more." I could hear Alexei Petrovich in the hall ordering the carriage to be brought round. I dashed headlong out of there, intending to return that evening to find out if anything had happened to them – whether they'd hurt themselves, or caught their death of cold, or drowned, or gone blind and so on. I arrived at about nine o'clock and gasped with astonishment: they looked so different! I was struck by their pale, gaunt faces, their dishevelled, unruly hair, their caked lips and lifeless expressions. Anyone not knowing the reason, might have thought that they had had to undergo some terrible ordeal – and indeed, without breaking the bounds of decency, they could well have been dancing the dance of death from *Robert*.* Mariya Alexandrovna was lying on her bed, hardly breathing; on the little table next to her lay countless numbers of little bottles and vials containing various spirits and other restorative and calming medicines. In the dining room the two infected servants, both equally pale and exhausted, were laying the table.

"Where have you been? What is the matter with you?" were my first questions.

"We've had a wonderful walk," Zurov replied, hardly able to catch his breath. "Let's tell you all about it."

"Wait a moment, calm down first: you seem at death's door."

"Hey! Let's have something to eat as quickly as possible! I'm dying to eat something."

"What, you want to have supper?"

"No, dinner."

"What do you mean, 'dinner'? Surely you've had dinner, haven't you?"

"Not yet. At first we didn't have the time: we walked and walked the whole time, and even got a little tired, and then, when we wanted to eat, the peasants only gave us some milk, and we'd only taken with us a few salty rolls, expecting to get back for dinner, so we didn't eat anything. But that's not really the point! It was such a wonderful walk!"

"Where did you go?"

"Beyond Srednyaya Rogatka.* There's a wonderful area there, a mile or so off the main road!"

"Oh, yes, so wonderful!" Mariya Alexandrovna agreed in a barely distinguishable voice, as she took a few drops. "Such views! I was so sorry you weren't there with us. Nature can be so fickle and yet so magnificent! You tell him, Zinaida... I can't."

"Picture to yourself," Zinaida began, "an enchantingly beautiful hillside above a little stream; on the hillside there are three pines and a birch tree – just as on Napoleon's grave, as Ivan Stepanych so appositely remarked; in the distance you can see a lake, now quivering in the wind like some muslin veil, now lying there quite still and motionless, like a mirror; all around it, on its banks, are clusters of little huts, seemingly about to dive down into the water – each of them little havens of unpretentious happiness, honest work, contentment, love and family virtues! Flung across the lake, from one steep bank to the other, built with extraordinary skill and boldness that would have been a credit to any engineer, there is a bridge of insubstantial stakes covered in... what is it called, *mon oncle?...** you told me a moment ago, but I've forgotten."

"In manure, my dear," the professor replied, "something really simple."

"Yes, that may well be so... anyway, it makes the landscape look especially attractive, reminiscent of Switzerland or China. Unfortunately even there, far from the crowds, nature is not totally free from man's impure footprint! Just imagine: in this lovely lake, unruffled by even the slightest breeze, there are soldiers washing their underclothes, covering the entire surface with soapsuds!"

"So this lake of yours is no larger than this room," I observed, "if its entire surface is covered in soapsuds."

"No, it's a little larger," Zurov replied, rather uncertainly.

"It's such wonderful weather at the moment," continued Zinaida Mikhailovna, "but it's twice as good there: unusually hot..."

"Yes, wonderfully hot," interjected Alexei Petrovich, "my mouth even went dry from the heat. Terrific! Fantastic! I love it when it's hot! I lost my hat on the way there, and fished bareheaded."

"No doubt out of respect for the fish," I said.

"No, there weren't any fish, just frogs popping up everywhere. But what does that matter? Don't you understand the sheer, undiluted pleasure of sitting and waiting for the float to suddenly start moving? You're such a heathen! You'll never understand such a divine feeling. For this, a coarse soul such as yours is no use at all: you need something a little more refined."

I asked Zinaida Mikhailovna to carry on, and she began again:

"And so we have this fantastic heat, as in the tropics – a totally open area, without any shade, nowhere to hide... could be Arabia! And the air! Just as in southern Italy! The scent of flowers everywhere, but once again the harmony of it all is ruined by the presence of man. In a place full of an abundance of sweet aromas, in which every blade of grass shelters a little insect rejoicing in life, where the breeze caresses every little flower, where our feathered friends chorus their hymn of praise to the Creator – even there, you will find people swaying and heaving like worms, engaged in their petty concerns that they have brought with them. Slaves themselves to contemptible profit and gain, they have humiliatingly enslaved nature for their own advantage. Just imagine: in this little corner of paradise they have begun building a... what sort of factory, *mon oncle*? I've forgotten once more."

"A factory for the production of lard," the old man replied. "You forget the most common things."

"That really wasn't nice at all!" complained Grandma. "The smoke nearly suffocated me – and, Lord save me, the smell!"

"Why do you take the old woman with you?" I asked under my breath. "She's only just recovered from her recent illness, and anyway she shouldn't be riding about everywhere at her age."

The old woman heard me.

"Why are you trying to stop them from taking me with them, my dear fellow?" she grumbled irritably. "I'm still alive, aren't I? What am I to do at home all day long?"

"Well, what about you children? How do you feel after the walk?"

"I've got a splitting headache from the heat, but it was great fun."

"And I would have loved it, except that I've felt sick all day."

"I've got this burning, itchy sensation on my face – can't touch it."

"And my stomach's played up the whole day, don't know why," they answered one after the other.

"And what about Verenitsyn? Was he with you?"

"Of course he was! He was the one who organized the whole trip."

"Where is he now then?"

"He's been carried home."

"What do you mean, 'carried home'?"

"He walked for such a long time that he lost the use of his legs."

"Goodness gracious! You do have wonderful walks, don't you? Can't you see now," I began to lecture them, "can't you understand what your destructive passion is doing to you? Surely you're aware that it's an illness, aren't you? Just look at you: Mariya Alexandrovna can hardly breathe; Zinaida Mikhailovna has become totally pale and has lost so much weight that it is seriously affecting her health and beauty; the children are at death's door; you yourself, Alexei Petrovich, have knocked at least ten years off your life. Stop doing this! No, really, I'm begging you to stop it!"

He gave me a thoughtful look, and he seemed to me to be acquiescing. I was overjoyed. "It's working!" I thought. "How about that! Just a few words!"

"Just you wait," he suddenly exclaimed, "and listen to what I have to say: as soon as my wife and children recover from this walk, we're going to organize a picnic and set off for Toksovo!"*

"Bravo! Bravissimo!" everyone roared in agreement. I made a gesture of dismissal, sighed and prepared to leave, with a tearful glance at Fyokla Alexeyevna.

"You must come with us – you absolutely have to!" Alexei Petrovich said to me. "Otherwise, you'll be in our bad books."

"Please come," Zinaida Mikhailovna implored, "or you'll get fat from laziness, like your friend Tyazhelenko, and you'll become as round as a ball."

"So what? Then I won't need to walk at all, but I'll simply be able to roll from place to place, which will be easier, I think."

The next morning, and in the following days, I received three notes reminding me about the picnic. The two lackeys, who had been afflicted with the disease, were constant visitors, associating with my own servants dangerously too much – something I found so alarming that, in order to nip the possibility of any infection in the bud, I went to the Zurovs myself to negotiate the details of the trip. Within a week everything was arranged. When I asked what I was to bring with me, they said I could bring what I liked.

At this point it occurred to me to make another attempt to save them. They had agreed on an isolated spot; there could easily be some disaster or another, and I was the only one not to be afflicted with the disease. Who would be there to respond, and how could I notify anyone in advance about the danger? Should I dash off to the head of police, put him fully in the picture and ask him to order a group of his men to lie in wait and observe, and then, if something disastrous should happen, give them a signal? But to confide in the head of police would mean that everybody would get to know about this malevolent disease, and I didn't want that. I decided to go and ask Tyazhelenko for his advice.

"But what are you afraid might happen, exactly?" he asked.

"Well, they might carelessly set the countryside ablaze, for example. You know how strangely they behave in those circumstances: they could set up the samovar, have a cigar and toss it away. I'm afraid that one of them could drown, or come to real harm. Who knows what could happen?"

"Hey, stop worrying, nothing of the sort's going to happen – they're aware what they're doing. Just watch that they don't go too far, don't catch cold, and, above all, that they don't go too long without food – that's the most important thing!"

"But how on earth can I keep an eye on them all just on my own? Do you know what, dear Nikon Ustinych? You were always one for a good deed, so why don't you stir your stumps for a change and come with me, just for a day?"

He gave me a stern glance and didn't say a single word. This didn't, however, deter me. I had another shot at trying to persuade him – and would you believe it! – by that evening I had succeeded in extracting an agreement out of him, on condition that I would provide him with food and a carriage.

On the appointed day, at seven o'clock in the morning, the two of us caught up with a charabanc at the entrance to the city. In it, apart from the Zurovs themselves, were seated the old professor with Zinaida Mikhailovna, while the children travelled behind in a carriage. Tyazhelenko had brought his favourite food with him, ham, while I had some confectionery and a bottle of Malaga.

We must have stopped at least eight times en route: now Mariya Alexandrovna wanted to sniff some little flowers on a mound of earth running alongside a building, now Alexei Petrovich thought there had to be a fish swimming around in a large puddle that had formed after the rain, and he started casting his fishing rod. While all this was going on, the children spent the whole time eating. But, just as everything on this earth has to come to an end sometime or other, so we finally arrived at some village, where we left the carriages, together with one of the servants – the other we took with us. Alexei Petrovich immediately went off somewhere with two of the elder children. Because of her blindness, Grandma was deposited on the grass near the village where we had stopped, and Tyazhelenko, having hardly covered a couple of a hundred yards, collapsed in exhaustion by her side. Leaving them both there, we ourselves set off, and, as they say in folk tales, walked and walked and walked, and there was no end to our walking – I'll only say that we walked down into five valleys, around seven lakes, clambered up three hills, sat under seventy-one trees in a large, dense forest and kept on stopping whenever we came across particularly remarkable spots.

"Goodness, what a terrifyingly gloomy abyss!" Mariya Alexandrovna remarked, looking down into a ravine.

"Oh yes!" Zinaida Mikhailovna added with a deep sigh. "It must have swallowed up more than one living creature in its time. Look: down at the bottom, in the gloom, you can see white bones!"

And, indeed, the skeletons of various noble beasts were scattered around at the bottom of the ravine – the bones of cats and dogs, among which Verenitsyn (who, as already has been said, had an absolute passion for exploring any and all ravines) was wandering around. At another spot my Feklusha, for ever imprinted on my mind, took it into her head to rhapsodize about nature.

"Let's climb that magnificent hill," she said, pointing to a mound of earth a couple of feet high. "There's sure to be a wonderful view from there."

We climbed the mound, only to find a fence, marking the boundary to a brick factory.

"People, nothing but people!" said a disgusted Zinaida Mikhailovna.

But at this point we were fated to experience a little disaster: Volodya jumped in the air and found himself at the bottom of a ditch. Mariya Alexandrovna bent down to him in alarm and suffered the same fate; Zinaida, equally alarmed and anticipating a disaster, went up to her knees in the ditch – something that she did practically every trip. Verenitsyn, one of the Zurovs' nephews and I hurried over to help and pulled them out in a pitiable condition: Volodya had a nosebleed, Mariya Alexandrovna had got herself covered in mud, while Zinaida Mikhailovna had to sit down on the bank and change her stockings, a spare pair of which she had by some miracle somehow managed to bring with her. There's foresight for you! Well, has it ever occurred to any of you, ladies and gentlemen, to show such prudence in such circumstances?... What can one say? Just what one would expect of the female sex!

We found all that walking utterly exhausting. My thoughts were turning to rest and food.

"Time for dinner," I said. "It's three o'clock."

"No, we'll drink some tea first," Mrs Zurov said, "and go back for dinner."

I stood there in disbelief, remembering that we had already walked some five miles from the village. The servant had brought a small samovar, together with some tea and sugar. Thank Heaven for small mercies! We were now just beginning to think where we were going to shelter for the night when, suddenly – thank the Lord! – a few hundred yards away we spied a windmill, by a little stream. No need to think what to do: that's where we'd go!

"Fate has been so kind to us!" Mariya Alexandrovna said. "I shall so enjoy drinking my tea, listening to the water rushing along! I shall imagine I'm listening to the Rhine flowing along, or that I'm on the banks of the Niagara... oh, if only I were there now, breathing in that air!"

"All in good time," Verenitsyn remarked quietly. I gave him an astonished look, but he fell silent and turned away from me. Utterly worn out, we finally managed to crawl to the mill. Covered in flour as a living symbol of his profession, a Chukhon met us in the doorway, holding his cap in his hand.

"If you'll allow us to stop and have a rest here, have some tea, it'll be worth your while."

"All right," he said listlessly.

We went in and took our various places on the flour-covered benches. We tried to start a conversation, but without success: annoyingly, tiredness and the noise made by the mill turning in the wind meant we were unable to say anything.

The servant came in with the samovar, and we asked the Chukhon for some cups. He went away for a moment and returned a minute later with a huge wooden bowl. We started to explain what it was we wanted, and the quick-witted Finn struck himself on the forehead and brought us a number of narrow, rather elongated glasses used by our peasants to propose toasts. I began to find this all rather amusing, but it only made everyone else angry. The ladies were reluctant to touch these vials of greenish glass, but there was nothing for it: we hadn't brought any cups with us, and necessity – unbearable thirst, that is – compelled us all to touch them not only with our hands, but even... horrible to say it now!... our lips. Just think: what strange things we are sometimes forced to touch through necessity! But at this point fate, it seems, took pity on us and decided not to force tender ladies' mouths coming into contact with anything untoward: Mariya Alexandrovna asked for tea, and Andrei produced a little casket; they opened it... and gasped with astonishment, horror and irritation: a metal snuffbox lay upside down, its lid open, on top of the tea; the unfortunate

Andrei had put it there by mistake, creating a mixture of tea and snuff! After a moment's silence, Mariya Alexandrovna and Zinaida Mikhailovna, who had been so looking forward to the tea, burst into tears; Feklusha tried to separate out the poisonous stuff, but its small grains had penetrated right down to the bottom of the casket, and, with it, our hearts. Andrei alone remained unperturbed by his own stupidity: when we tore into him with our reproaches, he said angrily:

"What's all the fuss about? What's so important about your tea? I've had a blow as well: I've lost all my snuff. I've done such things before: once, when travelling with a general, I put a candle in the pocket of his full dress uniform by mistake; it melted in the heat, and the wax spread everywhere, ruining his uniform. That was far more important than this, but even so I didn't lose much sleep over it!"

"How about something to eat, at least?" Verenitsyn asked the Finn. And this simple-hearted son of the soil brought us a few onions and some kvass in the aforesaid bowl, placing them on the table with a bow. The ladies recoiled in horror.

"Is that all?"

"There's flour," he said triumphantly. Our whole bodies aching from inexpressible tiredness, we set off back to the village; our throats and chests seemed to be on fire; and to cap it all, we had to take it in turns to carry the ladies. Just the time for me to attack them for embarking on such a trip in the first place! But I am nothing if not a generous soul, and I kept my anger hidden deep within me.

When our little refuge came into view, the crusaders would hardly have greeted the sight of the holy city with greater joy – but something then happened to dampen our delight. As we approached the village, we could hear the cry of familiar voices. "Help! Help!" Hurrying to see what the matter was, we saw Grandma and Tyazhelenko sitting on the grass, desperately trying to defend themselves from three hounds, which had already succeeded in playfully snatching the old woman's hat from her head, together with Tyazhelenko's peaked cap, and who continued to leap and romp around them, yelping and whining. Just at that moment the hunters emerged from a little copse and drove the dogs off.

Once order had been restored, Nikon Ustinovich gave me a look of mute reproach. The expression on his face betrayed a struggle between two emotions: justified indignation and an unsatisfied urge to eat.

"Dinner at five o'clock!" he exclaimed. "Have you ever heard the like!"

"We've had such a wonderful walk, *Monsieur Tiagelenko*!" said Zinaida Mikhailovna. "Such a pity you weren't with us!"

"You find the fact of my presence in this world particularly nauseating, of course," he replied with a bitter smile. "You would have been overjoyed to see me collapse lifeless on the spot as a result of all that walking – not to mention the fact I still haven't had a bite to eat!"

"Just a big ball," whispered Zinaida mockingly. The professor hastened to the village. Finally we reached the place from where we had set off, bearing all the signs of utter exhaustion.

"Food, food, as quickly as possible!" everyone shouted. All the infected people made a dash to have dinner on the meadow, but Tyazhelenko barred their way.

"You eat your meal on the meadow over my dead body!" he said, something that would have been physically difficult, and they therefore laid the table for the meal in the hut. Mariya Alexandrovna ordered that mustard, vinegar and other seasonings and dressings be placed on the table.

"Who brought the salad and the other cold food?" she asked. "Order it to be put on the table." Silence. "Why is nobody saying anything?"

"Probably because nobody brought it," I said.

"Well, then, let's start with the pâté. Let's have it, Andrei."

"But there isn't any pâté, my dear... the children ate it all on the way here."

I couldn't take my eyes off Tyazhelenko: his face had become suffused with a deathly pallor. He gave me a furious look.

"You have some ham, I think, Nikon Ustinych? What could be better?" Verenitsyn said. "Ask for it to be brought."

"The dogs you drove away ate it," Tyazhelenko said, by now totally exasperated.

"What's that, my dear man?" the old woman protested. "I'm sure I heard you chewing something long before the dogs turned up."

"No… it was just… just me eating your raisins."

"In any case, that's enough talk – let's have the broth."

"Nobody brought the broth, my lady."

"So we'll just have to eat *à la fourchette*," * the professor said. "Such a bitter fate, ladies and gentlemen! Let's move on to the hot dish. Who has brought a hot dish, and what is it?"

"I haven't brought any. Nor have I. Nor have I," the nine voices of all nine would-be picknickers chorused as one. The three remaining people – that is, Alexei Petrovich and the two children – were nowhere to be seen. Nobody had any idea where they had gone, and I was already beginning to mull over in my head the exact nature of the responsibilities I had placed on myself concerning the safety and wellbeing of sick people. But the relentless, sharp and piercing pangs of hunger eclipsed all other, less important, feelings – especially any of a philanthropic nature. As soon as it became clear that there had been no response to the request for hot food, everybody's heads sank onto their chests, and Nikon Ustinych, with a low groan, began hugging his stomach, as two friends sometimes embrace one another for mutual comfort when struck by one and the same catastrophe – and his stomach responded in sympathy with a pitiable rumbling.

"Which of us has got anything at all, then? Come on, everyone, speak up!" Mariya Alexandrovna demanded in a trembling voice. "You first, professor."

"I've got some Viennese pie and a bottle of Malaga," he replied.

Second voice: "I've got some sweets and a bottle of Malaga."

Third: "I've got two melons, a couple of dozen peaches and… a bottle of Malaga."

Fourth: "I've got some *crème au chocolat* and… a bottle of Malaga."

Fifth: "I've got some fruit syrup for the tea, an almond biscuit and… a bottle of Malaga."

Grandma: "I've got some raisins."

And up to eight voices confirmed that they had brought similar victuals with them, in each case accompanied by a bottle of Malaga.

"Good grief!" the professor said desolately. "Not a single bottle of Sauternes, not a drop of Madeira! Has there been some conspiracy or something for everyone to bring a bottle of Malaga?"

"No, just a simple coincidence."

"What do you mean, 'simple'? It's totally bizarre and really annoying!"

Finally a ninth voice put in shyly:

"I have some Parmesan cheese and a bottle of Lafitte."

All eyes turned immediately in the direction of the voice: it had been the melodious, heavenly voice of my darling, incomparable Feklusha. Oh! How irresistibly lovely she looked at that moment! I was jubilant as I noted the eagerness of that avaricious, unfeignedly avaricious crowd of people to place my heart's goddess on a pedestal and to bow down before her in that way. My blood surged within me like an ocean wave soaring to the sky; my heart pounded like an overwound pendulum clock. As I looked proudly around at everybody, I totally forgot about something for five minutes that was of extreme importance to me – the fact that I was starving. Say what you like: the moment of triumph of a beloved object is a divine moment! The professor kissed her hand with deep emotion; Mariya Alexandrovna embraced her exultant niece three times with a tenderness that was perfectly genuine; everyone else fervently showered her with the most flattering compliments; and Tyazhelenko, in a moment of high emotion, came out with the following memorable words:

"For the first time in my life I have been able to comprehend the true worth of a woman and to see the heights that she can achieve!"

But the joy was soon transformed into something that was not far short of tearful sobbing: the cheese amounted to no more than two and a half pounds, and nine mouths that had opened in such greedy anticipation snapped silently shut, and in some cases you could hear the grinding of teeth. Nikon Ustinovich scornfully pushed away the slice he was proffered and fell into a state of lethargic stupor. And indeed, to see all hope disappear when it is so nearly in your grasp is very hard to bear! Everyone lapsed into gloomy silence and sullenly started to set about the titbits, every so often taking sips of the Malaga. Towards the end of this highly unusual dinner, an exhausted Alexei Petrovich arrived, without his usual hat and gloves, and with two of the children and three yorsh.*

"Food! Food! For the love of God and all the saints, something to eat!" But all that remained was a little Malaga – its sickly sweetness merely mocking the fact that appetites had been outrageously unfulfilled, forming the prelude to the excruciating torture that is ravenous hunger.

Dinner concluded with a pitcher of milk. The Malaga, however, had had its usual effect: everyone cheered up, with Zinaida Mikhailovna becoming particularly merry. Getting up from the table, she began to click her dainty little fingers, stamp her little feet and jauntily start singing a variation of 'The Young Maiden at the Feast'.*

"For goodness' sake! You won't be able to stay on your feet, my dear!" her uncle said.

"I'm not sure I particularly need to!" she replied so charmingly, with such an enchanting smile and such a heady, intoxicating expression in her eyes that I was very nearly ready to grab her little hand and kiss it, but I didn't have the courage!

After dinner the Zurovs wanted to propose a walk. But realizing the time had come to act, I set about my sacred task with alacrity and eloquence.

"Stay where you are," I said, "and listen to me!" And I can say without boasting that I painted them with particular skill a convincing picture of their disastrous passion, with all its horrendous consequences. They listened to me attentively, exchanging glances with each other from time to time. I continued trying to convince them through sheer force of eloquence, as Peter the Hermit* had once done, but with the difference that he had tried to persuade, whereas I was setting out to dissuade; finally, I came to the catastrophe.

"You have been possessed by a hitherto unknown and unique disease, which has never been given a name, either in any other country, or here." At this point in my speech I particularly convincingly concentrated on the unattractive nature of it all, giving examples and reports from witnesses. "You have ruined your lives, been blinded, lured into an abyss and the person responsible for it all is right here, alive and breathing, sharing in your meal!! There he is!" I said, pointing to Verenitsyn.

Imagine the effect this remark had on everyone, dear reader! Remember a similar moment in Cicero's attack on Catiline.*

"There he is!" I repeated, emphasizing every word with great force. And... what do you think? Everybody was fast asleep. I very nearly blacked out. "Back to town!" I thundered in such an imperious voice that everyone leapt up simultaneously from their seats.

"No, out of town!" yelled Alexei Petrovich, still half asleep. In a commanding gesture I signalled to everyone that they should get moving. Within a moment the coachmen had harnessed the carriages.

"But that was such a wonderful walk, wasn't it?" Zurov and Verenitsyn both said as they climbed into their charabanc.

"Yes, and such a glorious spot!" added Mariya Alexandrovna and Zinaida Mikhailovna. "We had such fun! We must come here again another time."

We set off from the village at ten o'clock, reaching St Petersburg no earlier than 3 a.m. This time all attempts on the Zurovs' part to stop along the way – "to have a walk through the night-time dew", as Mariya and Zinaida kept on requesting – proved to be unsuccessful: in accordance with what we had already agreed, Tyazhelenko and I vehemently opposed any such suggestions.

As we drove up to the Voskresensky Bridge,* the leading carriage stopped. Fearing that the reason had to be some desire on the Zurovs' part for another out-of-town excursion, I was on the point of reminding them that we had already reached the city when suddenly the bridge appeared – or rather, didn't appear – in front of us.

"Where on earth is it?" I asked the policeman on duty.

"Can't you see, sir, that they've raised it?" he replied.

"And when are they going to lower it?"

"At about six o'clock."

"Allow me to congratulate you, *mesdames*: we can't get home, as the bridge has been raised!"

All the infected fellow travellers suddenly came alive.

"So we can go on an out-of-town excursion after all! Hey, Paramon! Turn back!"

Luckily the coachman was free of the disease, although he had long been suffering from extreme hunger and lack of sleep. He gave me a mournful look.

"Stay exactly where you are!" I said. Overjoyed, he leapt down from his box. Suddenly it started to drizzle; we had to look for shelter. Mariya Alexandrovna started crying from the cold; Zinaida Mikhailovna and the lovely Fyokla were scarcely able to breathe and kept on asking for something to eat and drink, but there was nothing available. The professor and Alexei Petrovich were sitting in the charabanc dozing off, and constantly bowing down to each other from the waist; every so often Tyazhelenko could be heard emitting low groans. Suddenly, Mariya Alexandrovna, who had listlessly been looking around at the surrounding houses, fixed her lorgnette on one particular sign, and her face lit up with joy.

"Oh, what a wonderful surprise!" she said. "Look, there's a pastry shop! We can sustain ourselves with food there and have a rest."

"Yes, you'll be able to eat your fill of pastries and have as much Malaga as you like," I replied, looking at the sign Mrs Zurov had been so overjoyed to see, which said: "FOOD AND TEA HERE".

"It's not a pastry shop," Zinaida Mikhailovna said excitedly. "It says there's food and tea."

"Perhaps chocolate as well!" Mariya Alexandrovna added.

"Brilliant!" everyone exclaimed. The men were very happy, thinking that they might be able to get a bite to eat, while the women had no idea that the establishment sporting this rather dubious sign was in fact an eating house of inferior quality, about which they had no conception whatsoever.

The rain now began to pour down in buckets, and we dashed under a most fortuitously placed sheltering roof. It was still very early; everyone was asleep in the eating house, meaning that it took considerable effort on our part to rouse the proprietors. Eventually a burly, balding man in a red shirt opened one half of the door and stood there gaping with astonishment on seeing such an unexpected type of visitor. He spent some time deciding whether or not to let us in, but when we explained to him our reason for being there, he opened both halves, with a great to-do and deep bows.

I shall not take it upon myself to describe the interior of an establishment of that sort, since just one fleeting glance will not suffice. I had actually never been there before – although, ever since the ladies (and what ladies they were: Mariya Alexandrovna and Zinaida Mikhailovna!) started visiting places of that kind I definitely wouldn't be ashamed to admit the fact. And no, I am afraid I'm not lying. In actual fact, anyone who loves wandering around the streets of St Petersburg will have at least a rough idea what is meant by an eating house, because they are to be found for the most part in the lower floors of houses, even basements, making it clear to the inquisitive eye exactly what type of establishment they are. What passer-by has not been struck by the sight of the pink or light-blue calico curtains framing their windows? If you were to look from the street directly through the door, you would always be able to see, in the depths of the room, a huge table laid with little glasses, carafes and plates with various titbits of food, with some bearded Ganymede* standing at the table; if you were to look through the window on a Sunday, you would undoubtedly be able to see a group of friends revelling and feasting, their faces glowing as if illumined by artificial gaslight; and the ribald laughter, the singing and the sound of the accordion would confirm that you would have found yourself not too far away from a temple of earthly delight. "What type of person frequents such an establishment?" you will ask. Oh reader, how can you be so obtuse? Have you never exited from a theatre or from some other place where you have left your heart for the following evening, have you never – I repeat – gone to the bourse and found there only horses and empty sleighs? And when you've shouted "Cabby!", don't you remember three or four of them suddenly appearing seemingly from nowhere? If this has happened to you, then it would have been from an eating house that they had suddenly emerged. Or why should the proprietor of a little shop opposite where you live frequently make himself scarce, leaving his business in the care of a mere lad? It is because there is an eating house next door. Or what about a retired officer, with a begging letter that nobody ever reads, to whom you have just given some money? Where do you think he goes? Why, to an eating house, of course. Not possessing a great deal of practical experience in this case, I have been unable to assemble enough facts and set them out in greater detail; there is, however, no need to despair: it is rumoured that two particularly prolific writers, one from Moscow, the other from St Petersburg, O——v and B——n,* are in possession of everything that one would ever need to know about the subject, which they themselves have researched in person and have long since prepared a substantial tome on the topic.

Unfortunately the early hour at which we repaired to this establishment meant that it was empty of the public, so that we were unable either to acquaint ourselves with its customs or with the mindset and penchants of its visitors. I felt particularly sorry for the ladies: their horizons are limited enough as it is, but they were now being deprived of the opportunity of assimilating a whole range of new and varied impressions.

"Please, sirs, if you please! This way, to the parlour!" mine host said, as he led us into a filthy little room with low ceilings, hung with portraits. These had all the same strange characteristic: they were of different women, each with the same face.

"Good God! Where on earth are we?" the ladies exclaimed, and started to retreat, but their exit was barred by a whole phalanx of hungry men, led by Tyazhelenko. So, like it or not, they had no choice but to go in.

"What can I order for you, sir? What can I get you, madam?" the obliging man continued. "We have everything. And please don't think that we are some sort of low-class establishment, so to speak. We hardly ever get cabbies here – we have the very best clientele... the valet from the general's house, for example, such a dependable gentleman, with a watch! And now the good Lord has brought you to our door! Welcome! We are delighted to see such guests!"

Alexei Petrovich interrupted him.

"We would like some food and something to drink."

"Of course, sir – anything you like."

"How about some hot chocolate?" Mariya Alexandrovna asked.

"No, milady – we don't have chicalate."

"Well, some coffee then!"

"We have the very best coffee – only, there isn't any cream: you're here rather early, milady... the Okhta* milk girl still hasn't been."

"So what *do* you have?"

"Every sort of the most wonderful vodka. There is pie... extremely tasty, with gravy, or jam. Freshly baked biscuits, beef galantine, lamb – absolutely everything, milady!"

The more he trumpeted the fact that he had everything, the less inclined we were to try anything he offered us. Only Tyazhelenko performed miracles with a slice of stale ham, while the others drank tea.

Having spent about an hour and a half there, we finally tore ourselves away from that den of discomfort, anxiety and other such grievous afflictions. Once we had safely crossed the bridge, which had in the mean time been lowered, I was able to breathe more easily. "They're hardly likely to do a trip like that again soon," I thought. "They have no doubt been greatly affected by that experience, together with the little talk I gave them." When we reached the spot where Tyazhelenko and I had to take our leave of the Zurovs and go back home, Alexei Petrovich ordered the coachman to stop and climbed out of the charabanc.

"My wife and I have the most humble request to make of you," he said.

"I am at your service. What can I do for you?"

"It's like this, you see: although we've had a wonderful walk, and it was all great fun and such a lovely place and all that, in order somehow to give you at least some idea of a *real* out-of-town excursion, my wife and I would like it so much if you could accompany us on Friday to Ropsha* – just a single destination. And on Saturday, Sunday and Monday, to Petergof, Oranienbaum and Kronstadt respectively.* We have chosen these particular destinations so as to give you as great an idea as possible of the variety of our trips. Up until now you have accompanied us only on dry land: it is high time you familiarized yourself with the sea."

"My God! They're incorrigible!" I exclaimed dejectedly. "Forgive me, Alexei Petrovich, I regret that I am unable to accept your invitation: I shall be leaving for the country on Wednesday and will be coming to say my farewells tomorrow."

"Oh no! That's so sad!" exclaimed Mariya Alexandrovna. "But do you know what? Why don't you spend tomorrow, your final day, with us on a trip out-of-town?"

I dashed to my carriage and raced home, without looking back.

I wasn't lying: circumstances were really compelling me to be away from St Petersburg for a long time, and I did indeed say my farewells to the Zurovs on the following day. But the thought that they could all perish if left to their own devices forced me to resort to extraordinary measures: a few hours before my departure I told an intelligent, experienced and understanding doctor the whole story, asking him to make himself known to them, and, if he could perhaps find some remedy to eradicate or at least blunt the effect of this "evil malady", then he would be able to keep me informed of any success in the mean time. Having thus entrusted the afflicted family to his care, I was able to leave the city and arrive in the countryside in a more cheerful frame of mind.

Two years passed without me hearing anything at all from the doctor. But one evening at the very end of this period I received, together with a whole pile of newspapers and journals, a letter with a black seal. I quickly opened it and… once again my eyes filled with tears, and my head, despite all my efforts to keep it upright, sank down on my chest. I won't undertake to describe what had happened, since I won't be able to gather my thoughts or find the words. Let me rather quote in full the extremely sad lines in the fateful letter concerning both the Zurovs and Tyazhelenko: the doctor had been great friends with the latter…

"It happened during the night of the 15th to the 16th March," the doctor wrote apropos of Tyazhelenko. "Bobolenko came running to me in alarm with the news that his master was not feeling 'at all well'; his eyes had become sunken and he had turned completely blue. I dashed to Nikon Ustinovich and indeed found him in a desperate state; he was unable to say a single word, merely quietly groaning. After four bloodlettings I was able to bring him round, but…" A few lines further down: "A second apoplectic stroke, following quickly after the first, proved to be fatal." And then about the Zurovs, on another page: "Presuming that their letter to me had simply been a joke, I went to call on them, having been away from town for a couple of weeks. But to my absolute astonishment I found every door in the house locked. Outside I came across the old servant Andrei, and when I asked him where they were, he replied that they'd gone to 'Chukhonya', thereby confirming what they themselves had said in their letter to me. Wishing to find out more details, I went to see one of their relatives, someone you know, a Mr Mebomeldrinov. He confirmed what Andrei had said, adding that the family's plan to go to Finland and then on to Switzerland had long been under consideration, but that they had skilfully managed to conceal this from everyone, including me, and that their aim was to make their way to America, where, in their words, nature was more inspiring, the air much more fragrant, the mountains much higher, where there was much less dust everywhere, and so on..."

Soon I myself returned to St Petersburg, where I learnt from that very same relative that they had indeed gone to America, with all their goods and chattels, and settled there. A long time later I happened to get to know a well-travelled Englishman who lived in America. He told me that he knew this family and about their passion for taking trips into the countryside, but that these had eventually ended in the saddest possible way. "One day," the Englishman concluded his story, "having stocked up with clothing, underclothing and supplies of food, they set off for the mountains, from which they were never to return."

REPROACH
EXPLANATION
FAREWELL*

(1843)

REPROACH

You're going! Can that possibly be true? What a frightful bore! Such a tedious idea! But everything about us now looks so jolly; everything looks green, everything is in blossom, nature is celebrating goodness knows what, and you're going! Your departure has always seemed to me to be such a distant, almost impossible event that I was able to dream it might never happen. And what do you think? You are actually, callously, brazenly going, leaving behind an adoring world and departing for a totally different and unfamiliar place, surrounded by a whole crowd of lovely companions!

And, most horribly of all, you have imposed on all those orphans whom you have abandoned such a terrible burden – to say, or perhaps even to write, *goodbye* to you! But you yourself have avoided doing that, because it's so upsetting and difficult to have to say that word to those whom you love. One's heart beats so strongly when preparing to say that word... it courses with blood as one tries so desperately, so tortuously to cast off the burden of having to say it, and one goes so pale in the act of actually saying it! One soon becomes aware, in fact, how impossible it is to say: one has, as it were, to *give birth* to it... the very idea of separation is so difficult, the heart has to struggle so hard to come to terms with it; sometimes, indeed, the act of giving birth can be fatal. You understand just how difficult it is, as I understand just how difficult giving birth can be, even though I have never given birth to anybody. You understand, and yet you demand something that is the epitome of cruelty and selfishness!

EXPLANATION

"Those whom you love…" I said… I have known you for eight years, but this is the first time it has occurred to me to ask: *how* do I love you? Passionately, deeply? No! I have never presumed to rise to heights that are inaccessible to me. With a filial love perhaps? But you are so different in age from my mother, and I am far too old to be your son. With a brotherly love? Too dry. As a friend? There can be no such thing as friendship between a man and a woman. So how, then, can I love you? I don't know, really I don't. My love for you has crept imperceptibly into my soul, gradually become stronger; its origins have become lost in your innumerable qualities and virtues, in the unlimited nature of my gratitude towards you. Some time or other I will be able to ascertain, at my leisure, the nature of my love for you, but for now neither you nor I have time for that. Your departure is taking up all your time; your departure is dominating all my thoughts; my tongue is merely repeating what my heart is saying: *I love you, I love you, I love you!*

FAREWELL

And what about you? Do you love me? No! It would be too terrifying to try to find out… but, anyway… find out what? How can you have space for me in your heart? It is already too occupied, too full. As in a sacred temple, it shines with an inextinguishable flame, eternally serving on the altar of love and friendship. The high priests have been chosen, a multitude of worshippers, all with such rich offerings. They have forestalled me – me, a stranger, bearing such a humble mite. These are people who are totally unreachable and chosen for all time: once you have become a member of this group, it is for ever! You try to join and they threaten you with: *what do you think you're doing?* Terrifying.

No! In saying *goodbye* to you, I am demanding neither love or friendship, merely *memories* and *habitual courtesies*. Farewell, but come back, come back as soon as you possibly can – and give me the space in your attention that you would give an old, well-worn book that you read ages ago, which you found a little boring perhaps, but the kind of thing that people turn to every evening, *out of habit*, like saying a prayer before going to sleep and, yawning, reading a few long-since familiar lines.

Notes

p. 3, *"Dear God!... with women?"*: A quotation from 'The Fair at Sorochyntsi', the first story in the collection *Evenings on a Farm Near Dikanka* (1829–32) by Nikolai Gogol (1809–52).

p. 3, *"Went into one room – found myself in another"*: A quotation from Act 1, Scene 4 of the comedy *Woe from Wit* (1823) by Alexander Griboyedov (1795–1829).

p. 3, *"Blessed be the gathering dusk!" said Pushkin*: A quotation from Chapter 6 (xxi, l. 14) of Pushkin's *Eugene Onegin*.

p. 20, *"woe from wit"*: See second note to p. 3.

p. 23, *Gumbs, Junker and Plincke*: Expensive and fashionable St Petersburg shops. Gumbs' furniture shop was located on Italyanskaya Street; Junker's prints shop was on Nevsky Prospekt; Nicholls and Plinke's "English shop", selling various articles, was located on Bolshaya Morskaya Street, not far from Nevsky Prospekt.

p. 23, *the Works of Figlyarin*: Figlyarin is a nickname of Faddey Bulgarin (1789–1859), which came into use after Pushkin's 1830 epigram 'On Bulgarin' ("A Pole? Indeed! It's no disgrace: / Great Mickiewicz – he was one. / So why not join the Tatar race / Or call yourself a Jew for fun? I name you now (poor living lie): / 'Vidocq Figlyarin' – fool and spy!" – translation by John Coutts). Bulgarin was a man of Polish-Belorussian birth who was brought to St Petersburg as a child, trained as a cadet, then served for a while as a junior officer in the Russian army, before returning to Poland. After the Russian alliance with Napoleon following the Peace of Tilsit (1807), Bulgarin enlisted with the French army and fought with the French during the last phase of the Napoleonic Wars, then settled once more in Poland. In 1819 he finally took up residence in St Petersburg, gaining entry to the literary world there and becoming a prolific author, journalist, editor and critic. After the accession of Nicholas I and the suppression of the Decembrist uprising in 1825, Bulgarin began to work as an agent for the secret police. From the later 1820s he was an increasingly bitter literary rival and personal enemy of Pushkin, who had various nicknames for him, such as (Vidocq) Figlyarin.

p. 25, *Victor Hugo's expression, he had two knees on each leg*: The reference is to Victor Hugo's 1829 novel *The Last Day of a Condemned Man* (Chapter 48): "My steps were feeble, I sagged as if each of my legs had two knees."

p. 25, *shaking off the dust from his feet*: That is, break off all relations with Yelena. The expression derives from Matthew 10:14: "And whosoever shall not receive you, nor hear your words, when ye depart out of that house or city, shake off the dust of your feet."

p. 30, *magic mirror... Armida*: Armida is a beautiful Saracen warrior sorceress in Tasso's epic poem *Jerusalem Delivered*. Armida is about to murder a sleeping Christian soldier, Rinaldo, but instead she falls in love. She creates an enchanted garden where she holds him a lovesick prisoner. Eventually two of Rinaldo's fellow Crusaders find him and hold a shield to his face, so he can see his image and remember who he is.

p. 32, *as Pushkin did in his Eugene Onegin*: Onegin's arrival at a ball in St Petersburg is described in the first chapter of Pushkin's *Eugene Onegin* (XXVII ff.).

p. 39, *fleurs d'orange, des sels*: "Orange blossom, smelling salts" (French).

p. 40, *"Faites ce qu'il vous demande, je le veux bien!"*: "Do what he asks, I'm happy about it" (French).

p. 46, *(you will have noticed... from cups)*: This note is for our female readers (GONCHAROV'S NOTE).

p. 53, *both in the heavens above and on the earth below*: A reference to Exodus 20:4.

p. 55, *state councillor*: Fifth in the civil-service section of the Table of Ranks instituted by Peter the Great in 1722 (see front matter), the equivalent of the military rank of brigadier. There were fourteen ranks in total, and the Table remained in force until the 1917 revolution. Goncharov himself retired from the civil service in 1867 as Actual State Councillor, the fourth rank, equivalent to a major general.

p. 55, *the St Anna Medal*: The Russian Imperial Order of St Anna was established in 1735, with medals awarded for meritorious service.

p. 55, *Little Russian landowner*: Little Russia was a term, now obsolete, for eastern Ukraine.

p. 56, *Tyazhelenko… not worth the effort*: Tyazhelenko is the prototype for the lazy character Oblomov, the eponymous hero of Goncharov's greatest novel, published in 1859.

p. 56, *the Tauride Garden*: A landscaped park in the centre of St Petersburg, created in the 1780s, during the reign of Catherine the Great.

p. 61, *the Roman emperor Vitellius*: Aulus Vitellius (15–69 AD), Roman Emperor for eight months in 69 AD.

p. 62, *Petergof and Pargolovo*: Suburbs of St Petersburg.

p. 63, *Haymarket Square*: A large square in the centre of St Petersburg. Established in the 1730s, it quickly became the cheapest and most active market in the city.

p. 64, *he'll set off from Gorokhovaya Street… and so back to Gorokhovaya*: A walk encompassing an extremely large area of St Petersburg, from the centre up to the relatively uninhabited islands north of the city and back again.

p. 65, *the Kievan caves*: The reference is to the Kyivo-Perchers'ka Lavra (the Kiev Monastery of the Caves), one of the holiest centres of Eastern Orthodox Christianity, dating back to the early eleventh century.

p. 66, *the Orenburg area*: The city of Orenburg and its administrative region lie some 900 miles to the south-east of Moscow, close to the border with Kazakhstan.

p. 66, *Kalmyk*: The Kalmyks are an ethnic Mongol group living in the south of Russia.

p. 68, *the Summer Garden*: An island between the Neva, Fontanka and Moika rivers in the centre of St Petersburg. It shares its name with the adjacent Summer Palace of Peter the Great.

p. 71, *Theocritus*: The Greek bucolic poet Theocritus (d. *c*.260 BC).

p. 72, *Chukhna*: The Chukhna were a Finnish ethnic group living in the St Petersburg area of Russia.

p. 73, *Strelna... palace and the park*: The Konstantin Palace and the surrounding park were located in Strelna, a settlement along the Gulf of Finland near St Petersburg.

p. 77, *Robert*: A reference to *Robert le diable*, an opera by the German composer Giacomo Meyerbeer (1791–1864), first performed in 1831.

p. 77, *Srednyaya Rogatka*: A historically interesting area of St Petersburg, to the south of the city.

p. 78, *mon oncle*: "Uncle" (French).

p. 80, *Toksovo*: A settlement some fifteen miles to the north of St Petersburg, on the Karelian isthmus.

p. 87, *to eat à la fourchette*: "To have a light meal" (French).

p. 89, *yorsh*: A popular Russian cocktail, consisting of ten parts beer and one vodka.

p. 89, *'The Young Maiden at the Feast'*: A Russian folk song.

p. 90, *Peter the Hermit*: The French Roman Catholic priest Peter of Achères (1050–1115), a key figure in the People's Crusade of 1096.

p. 90, *Cicero's attack on Catiline*: In 63 BC the Roman statesman, writer and philosopher Marcus Tullius Cicero (106–43 BC) famously accused a fellow senator, Lucius Sergius Catilina (c.108–62 BC), of plotting to overthrow the Senate.

p. 91, *Voskresensky Bridge*: The second oldest bridge in St Petersburg, built across the River Neva in 1786. Originally a wooden pontoon structure, it was removed some hundred years later. Bridges across the Neva were (and still are) raised at night-time during the summer according to a particular schedule, to allow for the navigation of ships.

p. 93, *Ganymede*: The cup-bearer to the Gods in Greek mythology.

p. 93, *O——v and B——n*: Possibly a humorous allusion to the anarchists Nikolai Ogarev (1813–77) and Mikhail Bakunin (1814–76).

p. 94, *Okhta*: A historic region of St Petersburg, on the right bank of the River Neva.

p. 95, *Ropsha*: A settlement and favourite area for fishing and hunting some thirty miles to the south-west of St Petersburg.

p. 95, *Petergof, Oranienbaum and Kronstadt*: The town of Oranienbaum
is located on the Baltic coast to the west of St Petersburg. Kronstadt
is a town and naval base situated on Kotlin Island in the Baltic, some
nineteen miles to the west of the city.

p. 99, *Reproach. Explanation. Farewell*: Goncharov's message of farewell
possesses a semi-epistolary, semi-literary nature and is addressed
to Yevgeniya Petrovna Maykova (1803–80), who, together with her
husband, her two sons Valerian and Leonid and an acquaintance, left
St Petersburg for France and Germany on 15th June 1843. Goncharov
and Yevgeniya Petrovna had known each other for many years, writing
long letters to each other of an intimate, confidential nature.

For our complete list and latest offers

visit

almabooks.com/evergreens

GREAT POETS SERIES

Each volume is based on the most authoritative text, and reflects Alma's commitment to provide affordable editions with valuable insight into the great poets' works.

Selected Poems
Blake, William
ISBN: 9781847498212
£7.99 • PB • 288 pp

The Rime of the Ancient Mariner
Coleridge, Samuel Taylor
ISBN: 9781847497529
£7.99 • PB • 256 pp

Complete Poems
Keats, John
ISBN: 9781847497567
£9.99 • PB • 520 pp

Paradise Lost
Milton, John
ISBN: 9781847498038
£7.99 • PB • 320 pp

Sonnets
Shakespeare, William
ISBN: 9781847496089
£4.99 • PB • 256 pp

Leaves of Grass
Whitman, Walt
ISBN: 9781847497550
£8.99 • PB • 288 pp

MORE POETRY TITLES

Dante Alighieri: *Inferno, Purgatory, Paradise, Rime, Vita Nuova, Love Poems*;
Alexander Pushkin: *Lyrics Vol. 1 and 2, Love Poems, Ruslan and Lyudmila*;
François Villon: *The Testament and Other Poems*; Cecco Angiolieri: *Sonnets*;
Guido Cavalcanti: *Complete Poems*; Emily Brontë: *Poems from the Moor*;
Anonymous: *Beowulf*; Ugo Foscolo: *Sepulchres*; W.B. Yeats: *Selected Poems*;
Charles Baudelaire: *The Flowers of Evil*; Sándor Márai: *The Withering World*;
Antonia Pozzi: *Poems*; Giuseppe Gioacchino Belli: *Sonnets*; Dickens: *Poems*

WWW.ALMABOOKS.COM/POETRY

ALMA CLASSICS

ALMA CLASSICS aims to publish mainstream and lesser-known European classics in an innovative and striking way, while employing the highest editorial and production standards. By way of a unique approach the range offers much more, both visually and textually, than readers have come to expect from contemporary classics publishing.

www.almaclassics.com